Albert Taylor Bledsoe

An Examination of President Edward's Inquiry

Albert Taylor Bledsoe

An Examination of President Edward's Inquiry

1st Edition | ISBN: 978-3-75238-207-5

Place of Publication: Frankfurt am Main, Germany

Year of Publication: 2020

Outlook Verlag GmbH, Germany.

Reproduction of the original.

AN EXAMINATION

OF

PRESIDENT EDWARDS' INQUIRY

·

BY
ALBERT TAYLOR BLEDSOE.

1

INTRODUCTORY REMARKS.

I ENTERED upon an examination of the "Inquiry" of President Edwards, not with a view to find any fallacy therein, but simply with a desire to ascertain the truth for myself. If I have come to the conclusion, that the whole scheme of moral necessity which Edwards has laboured to establish, is founded in error and delusion; this has not been because I came to the examination of his work with any preconceived opinion. In coming to this conclusion I have disputed every inch of the ground with myself, as firmly and as resolutely as I could have done with an adversary. The result has been, that the views which I now entertain, in regard to the philosophy of the will, are widely different from those usually held by the opponents of moral necessity, as well as from those which are maintained by its advocates.

The formation of these views, whether they be correct or not, has been no light task. Long have I struggled under the stupendous difficulties of the subject. Long has darkness, a deep and perplexing darkness, seemed to rest upon it. Faint glimmerings of light have alternately appeared and disappeared. Some of these have returned at intervals, while others have vanished for ever. Some have returned, and become less wavering, and led on the mind to other regions of mingled obscurity and light. Gladly and joyfully have I followed.

By patient thought, and sustained attention, these faint glimmerings have, in more instances than one, been made to open out into what has appeared to be the clear and steady light of truth. If these are not mere fond illusions, the true intellectual system of the world is far different from that which has been constructed by the logic of President Edwards.

If his system be false, why, it may be asked, has the Inquiry so often appeared to be unanswerable? Why has it been supposed, even by some of the advocates of free agency, that logic is in favour of his system, while consciousness only is in favour of ours? One reason of this opinion is, that it has been taken for granted, that either the scheme of President Edwards or that of his opponents must be true; and hence, his system has appeared to stand upon immoveable ground, in so far logic is concerned, only because he has, with such irresistible power and skill, demolished and trampled into ruins that of his adversaries. Reason has been supposed to be on his side, because he has so clearly shown that it is not on the side of his opponents. But the scheme of the motive-determining power, does not necessarily arise out of the ruins of the self-determining power; it is only to the imagination that it appears to do so. Because the one system is false, it does not follow that the other is true.

There is another and still more powerful reason for the idea in question. The advocates of free agency have granted too much. The great foundation principles of the scheme of moral necessity have been incautiously admitted by its adversaries. These principles have appeared so obvious at first view, that their correctness has not been doubted; and hence they have been assumed by the one side and conceded by the other. Yet, if I am not greatly mistaken, they have been derived, not from the true oracles of nature, but from what Bacon quaintly calls the "idols of the tribe." If this be the case, as I think it will hereafter appear to be; then in order to secure a complete triumph over the scheme of moral necessity, even on the arena of logic, we must not only know *how to reason*, but also *how to doubt*.

I fully concur with the younger Edwards, that "Clarke, Johnson, Price, and Reid have granted too much;" and while I try to show this, I shall also endeavour to show that President Edwards has assumed too much, not for the good of the cause in which he is engaged, but for the attainment of truth.

If his system had not been founded upon certain natural illusions, by which the true secrets of nature are concealed from our view, it could never have been the boast of its admirers, "that a reluctant world has been constrained to bow in homage to its truth." If we would try the strength of this system then, we must bend a searching and scrutinizing eye upon the premises and assumptions upon which it is based; we must put aside every preconceived notion, even the most plausible and commonly received opinions, and lay our minds open to the steady and unbiased contemplation of nature, just as it has been created by the Almighty Architect; we must view the intellectual system of the world, not as it is seen through our hasty and careless conceptions, but as it is revealed to us in the light of consciousness and severe meditation. This will be no light task, I am aware; but whosoever would seek the truth on such a subject, must not expect to find it by light and trifling efforts; he must go after it in all the loving energy of his soul. Let this course be pursued, honestly and perseveringly pursued, and I am persuaded, that a system of truth will be revealed to the mind, to which it will not be constrained to render "a reluctant homage," but which, by harmonizing the deductions of logic with the dictates of nature, will secure to itself the most pleasing and delightful homage of which the human mind is susceptible.

Those false conceptions which are common to the human mind, those "idols of the tribe," of which Bacon speaks, have been, as it is well known, the sources of some of the most obstinate errors, both in science and in religion, that have ever infested the world. And it is evident, that while the assumptions from which any system, however false, legitimately results, are conceded, it will stand, like a wall of adamant, against the most powerful artillery of logic. It will remain triumphant in spite of all opposition. It may be contrary to our natural convictions, and consequently liable to our suspicions; but it cannot be refuted by argument. Its advocates may reason correctly, and its adversaries may appeal to opposite truths; but neither can ever arrive at the truth, and the whole truth. This has appeared to me to be the case, with respect to the long controverted question of liberty and necessity.

The above causes, conspiring with some instances of false logic, which have been overlooked amid so much that is really conclusive, and also with a number of unsound, yet plausible, devices to reconcile the scheme of moral necessity with the reality of virtue and free-agency, have, in the minds of many, rendered the work of President Edwards both an acceptable and an unanswerable production. Such, at least, is the conclusion to which I have been constrained to come; but whether this conclusion be correct or not, it is not for me to determine. Time alone can show, whether the foundation of his system, like that of truth, is immutable, or whether, like many which have been laid by the master spirits of other ages, it is destined to pass away, though not to be forgotten.

In the above enumeration of causes I have not alluded to those of a theological nature; because they have been but partial in their operation. And besides, I have not wished to refer to this subject at all, except in so far as, is necessary to indicate wherein I conceive the errors of the Inquiry to consist, and thereby to point out the course which I intend to pursue in the following discussion.

SECTION I.

It is worse than a waste of time, it is a grievous offence against the cause of truth, to undertake to refute an author without having taken pains to understand exactly what he teaches. In every discussion, the first thing to be settled is the point in dispute; and if this be omitted, the controversy must needs degenerate into a mere idle logomachy. It seldom happens that any thing affords so much satisfaction, or throws so much light on a controversy, as to have the point at issue clearly made up, and *constantly borne in mind.*

What then, is the precise doctrine of the Inquiry which I intend to oppose? The great question is, says Edwards, what determines the will. It is taken for granted, on all sides, that the will is determined; and the only point is, or rather has been, as to what determines it. It is determined by the strongest motive, says one; it is not determined by the strongest motive, says another. But although the issue is thus made up in general terms, it is very far from being settled with any tolerable degree of clearness and precision; ample room is still left for all that loose and declamatory kind of warfare in which so many controversialists delight to indulge.

The question still remains to be settled, what is meant by determining the will? In regard to this point, the necessitarian does not seem to have a very clear and definite idea. "The object of our Inquiry," says President Day, "is not to learn whether the mind acts at all. This no one can doubt. Nor is it to determine *why we will at all.* The very nature of the faculty of the will implies that we put forth volitions. But the real point of inquiry is, *why we will one way rather than another; why we choose one thing rather than its opposite,*" p. 42. One would suppose from this statement, that we have nothing to do with the question, *why we put forth volitions,* but exclusively with the question, why we will *one way rather than another.* Here the author's meaning seems to be plain, and we may imagine that we know exactly where to find him; but, in the very next sentence, he declares that the object of our inquiry is, "what is it that determines *not only that there shall be volitions,* but what they shall be?" p. 42. In one breath we are told, that we have nothing to do with the question, why our volitions are put forth or come into existence; these are admitted to be implied in the "very nature of the faculty of the will;" but, in the very next, we are informed that we have to inquire into this point also. One moment, only one of these points is in dispute, and the next, both are put in controversy. Surely, this does not indicate any very clear and definite idea, on the part of President Day, as to the point at issue.

The notion of President Edwards, on this subject, appears to be equally unsteady and vacillating. "Thus," says he, "by determining the will, if the phrase be used with any meaning, *must be intended*, causing that the act of the *will should be thus, and not otherwise:* and the will is said to be determined, when, in consequence of some action, or influence, its choice is directed to, and fixed upon a particular object. As when we speak of the determination of motion, we mean causing the motion of the body to be in such a direction, rather than another," p. 18.

Now, are we to understand from this, that the determination of the will can only refer to the question, why it is directed to and fixed upon a particular object, and not to the question, how it comes to put forth a volition at all? One would certainly suppose so; and that, according to Edwards, we have nothing to do with the question, "How a spirit comes to act," but with the question, "why its action has such and such a particular direction and determination." But this supposition would be very far from the truth. For he informs us, that "the question is not so much, How a spirit endowed with activity comes to act, as why it exerts such an act, and not another; or why it acts with such a particular determination?" This clearly implies, that although the question, "How a spirit comes to act," is not chiefly concerned in the present controversy; yet *it is partly* concerned in it. This question is concerned in it, though not *so much* as the other question, why the act of the mind is as it is, rather than otherwise.

This is not all. When Edwards attacks the doctrine of his adversaries, in regard to the determining of the will, he never seems to dream of the idea, which, according to himself, if the phrase mean any thing, *must* be attached to it. He treats it as a settled point, that by determining the will must be intended, not causing volition to be one way rather than another, but causing it to come into existence. He could take this expression to mean the one thing or the other, just as it suited his purpose.

Are these two questions really distinct? Can there be one cause of volition, and another cause of its particular direction? I answer, there cannot. No such distinction can be shown to exist by a reference to the cause of motion. Force is the cause of motion. One force may put a body in motion; and, afterwards, another force may change the direction of its motion. Upon a superficial observation, this may seem to illustrate the distinction in question; but, upon more mature reflection, it will not appear to do so. For the force which sets a body in motion necessarily causes it to move in one particular direction, and not another; because it is impossible for a body to move without moving in a particular direction. After one force has put a body in motion, another force, it is true, may change its direction; but in such a case, it is not correct to say, that one force caused its motion and another the direction of that motion. For, in reality, both the motion of the body and its direction, result from the joint action of the two forces; or, in other words, each force contributes to the motion, and each to its direction. Both the motion and its direction are caused by what is technically called, in mechanical philosophy, the "resultant" of the two forces; and the case is really not different, so far as the distinction in question is concerned, from the case of motion produced by the action of a single force. The absurdity of this distinction consists, in supposing that a body may be put in motion without moving in a particular direction; and that something else beside the cause of its motion, is necessary to account for the direction of that motion. The illustration, therefore, drawn from the phenomena of motion, fails to answer the purpose for which President Edwards has produced it.

The same absurdity is involved in the supposition, that one thing may cause volition to exist, and another may cause it to be directed to and fixed upon a particular object. No man can conceive of a choice as existing, which has not some particular object. It is of the very nature and essence of a choice to have some particular direction and determination. If a choice exists at all, it must be a choice of some particular thing. Hence, whatever causes a volition to exist, must cause it to have a particular direction and determination. Let any one show a choice, which is not the preference of one thing rather than another, and then we may admit that there is some reason for the distinction in question; but until then, we must be permitted to regard it as having no foundation in the nature of things. If it were necessary, this matter might be fully and unanswerably illustrated; but a bare statement of it is sufficient to render it perfectly clear.

We shall hereafter see, that the reason why President Edwards supposed that there is some foundation for such a distinction is, that he did not sufficiently distinguish between the cause of a thing and its condition. Although we may suppose that the "activity of the soul" is the cause of its acting; yet motive may be the indispensable condition of its acting; and, in this sense, may be the reason why a volition is one way rather than another. But it is denied that there can be two *causes* in the case; one to produce volition, and another to determine its object. We have seen that such a supposition is absurd; and we shall hereafter see, that Edwards was led to make it, by confounding the condition with the cause of volition.

After all, it may be said, that Edwards himself did not really consider these two things as distinct, but only as different aspects of the same thing. If so, it will follow, that when he undertook to establish his own scheme, he represented motive as the cause of volition; and yet when he was reminded, that the activity of the nature of the soul is the cause of its actions, he replied, that although this may be very true, yet this activity of nature is not the "cause why its acts are thus and thus limited, directed and determined." He replied that the question is not *so much*, "How a spirit comes to act," as why it acts thus, and not otherwise. That is to say, it will follow, that he chose to build up his scheme under one aspect of it, and to defend it under another aspect thereof; that as the architect of his system, he chose to assume and occupy the position, that motive is the cause of volition itself; yet as the defender of it, he sometimes preferred to present this same position under the far milder aspect, that although "the activity of spirit, may be the cause why it acts," yet motive is the cause why its acts are thus and thus limited, &c. In other words, it will follow, that his doctrine possesses two faces; and that with the one it looks sternly on the scheme of necessity, whilst, with the other, it seems to smile on its adversaries.

The truth is, the great question which President Edwards discusses throughout the Inquiry, as we shall see, is "How a spirit comes to act;" and the other question, "why its action is thus and thus limited," &c., which, on occasion, swells out into such immense importance, as to seem to cover the whole field of vision, generally shrinks down into comparative insignificance. As a general thing, he goes along in the even tenor of his way, to prove that no event can begin to be without a cause of its existence; and, in particular, that no volition can come into existence without being caused to do so by motive; and it is only when it is urged upon him, that "a spirit endowed with activity" may give rise to its own acts, that he takes a sudden turn and reminds us, that the question is not so much "how a spirit comes to act?" as "why its acts are thus and thus limited?"

From the supposition made by Edwards, that "if activity of nature be the cause why a spirit acts," it has been concluded that he regarded the soul of man as the efficient cause of its volitions, and motive as merely the occasion on which they are put forth or exerted. But surely, those who have so understood the Inquiry, have done so very unadvisedly, and have but little reason to complain, as they are prone to do, that his opponents do not understand him. If Edwards makes mind the efficient cause of volition, what becomes of his famous argument against the self-determining power, by which he reduces it to the absurdity of an infinite series of volitions? "If the mind causes its volition," says he, "it can do so only by a preceding volition; and so on *ad infinitum.*" Is not all this true, on the supposition that the mind is the efficient cause of volition? And if so, how can any reader of Edwards, who does not wish to make either his author or himself appear ridiculous, seriously contend that he holds mind to be the efficient, or producing cause of volition? There be pretended followers and blind admirers of President Edwards, who, knowing but little of his work themselves, are ever ready to defend him, whensoever attacked, even by those who have devoted years to the study of the Inquiry, by most ignorantly and flippantly declaring that they do not understand him. These pseudo-disciples will not listen to the charge, that Edwards makes the strongest motive the producing cause of volition; but whether this charge be true or not, we shall see in the following section.

SECTION II.

OF EDWARDS' USE OF THE TERM CAUSE.

WE have already seen that Edwards must be understood as holding motive to be the cause of volition; but still we cannot make up the issue with him, until we have ascertained in what sense he employs the term *cause*. It has been contended, by high authority, that he did not regard motive as the efficient, or producing cause of volition, but only as the occasion or condition on which volition is produced. Hence, it becomes necessary to examine this point, and to settle the meaning of the author, in order that I may not be supposed to misrepresent him, and to dispute with him only about words.

The above notion is based on the following passage:

"I would explain," says President Edwards, "how I would be understood when I use the word *cause* in this discourse; since, for want of a better word, I shall have occasion to use it in a sense which is more extensive, than that in which it is sometimes used. The word is often used in so restrained a sense as to signify only that which has a positive efficiency or influence to produce a thing, or bring it to pass. But there are many things which have no such positive productive influence; which yet are causes in this respect, that they have truly the nature of a reason why some things are, rather than others; or why they are thus rather than otherwise."... . "I sometimes use the word *Cause*, in this Inquiry, to signify any antecedent, either natural or moral, ... upon which an event so depends, that it is the ground or reason, either in whole or in part, why it is, rather than not; or why it is as it is, rather than otherwise; or, in other words, any antecedent with which a consequent event is so connected, that it truly belongs to the reason why the proposition which affirms that event, is true; whether *it has any positive influence, or not*. And, agreeably to this, I sometimes use the term *effect* for the consequence of another thing, which is perhaps rather an occasion than cause, most properly speaking." And he tells us, that "I am the more careful thus to explain my meaning, that I may cut off occasion, from any that might seek occasion to cavil and object against some things which I may say concerning the dependence of all things which come to pass, on some cause, and their connection with their cause," p. 50-1.

This is the portion of the Inquiry on which the younger Edwards founds his conclusion, that his father did not regard motive as the *efficient* cause of volition, but only as the occasion, or condition, or antecedent of volition. He finds this language in the Essays of Dr. West; "We cannot agree with Mr. Edwards in his assertion, that motive is the cause of volition;" and he replies,

11

"Mr. Edwards has very particularly informed us in what sense he uses the term *cause*;" and, in proof of this, he proceeds to quote a portion of the above extracts from the Inquiry. Having done this, he triumphantly demands, "Now, does Dr. West deny, that motive is an antecedent, on which volition, either in whole or in part depends? or that it is a ground or reason, either in whole or in part, either by positive influence or not, why it is rather than not? Surely, he cannot with consistency deny this, since he says, 'By motive we understand the *occasion*, end or design, which an agent has in view when he acts.' So that, however desirous Dr. West may be to be thought to differ, in this point, from President Edwards, it appears that he most exactly agrees with him," p. 65.

Now, if Edwards really believed that motive is merely the occasion on which the mind acts, agreeing herein most perfectly with Dr. West, why did he not say so? Why adhere to the term cause, which can only obscure such an idea, instead of adopting the word occasion, or condition, or antecedent, which would have clearly expressed it? Surely, if Edwards maintained the doctrine ascribed to him, he has been most unfortunate in his manner of setting it forth; it is a great pity he did not give it a more conspicuous place in his system. It is to be regretted, that he has not once told us that such was his doctrine, in order that we might see for ourselves his agreement with Dr. West in this respect, instead of leaving it to the initiated few to enlighten us on this subject.

He has, we are told, "very particularly informed us in what sense he uses the word cause," p. 64. Now is this so? Has he informed us that by *cause* he means *occasion?* He has done no such thing, and his language admits of no such construction. He merely tells us, that he *sometimes* uses the term cause to signify an occasion only; but when and where he so employs it, he has not explained at all. He has not once said, that when he applies it to motive he uses it in the sense of an occasion, or antecedent; and, if he had said so, it would not have been true. The truth is, that he has used the word in question with no little vagueness and indistinctness of meaning; for he sometimes employs it to signify merely an occasion, which exerts no positive influence, and sometimes to signify a producing cause. This is the manner in which he uses it, when he applies it to motive. In his definition of motive, as the younger Edwards truly says, he includes "*every cause* or occasion of volition;" every thing which has a "tendency to volition;" &c., p. 104. Thus, according to the younger Edwards himself, the elder Edwards has, in his definition of motive, included every conceivable cause of volition; and yet, when Dr. West objects that he makes motive the producing cause of volition, the very same writer replies that he has done no such thing: that he has "very

12

particularly explained in what sense he uses the word cause" when applied to motive, and that he means "by *cause*, no other than *occasion, reason, or previous circumstance necessary for volition*; and that in this Dr. West entirely agrees with him," p. 65. If we may believe the younger Edwards, then, when the author of the Inquiry says, that motive is the cause of volition, he means that it is no other than the occasion or previous circumstance necessary to volition, and not that it is the cause thereof in the proper sense of the word; and yet that it is the cause thereof in every conceivable sense of the word! Now, he agrees with Dr. West himself; and again, he teaches precisely the opposite doctrine! Let those who so fondly imagine that they are the only men who understand the Inquiry, and that the most elaborate replies to it may be sufficiently refuted by raising the cry of "misconstruction;" let them, I say, take some little pains to understand the work for themselves, instead of merely giving echo to the blunders of the younger Edwards.

President Edwards says, that the term cause is often used in so restrained a sense as to signify that which has "a *positive efficiency* or *influence* to *produce* a thing, or bring it to pass." It is in this restrained sense that I use the word, when I say that President Edwards regarded motive as the cause of volition; and it is in this sense that I intend to make the charge good. I intend to show that he regarded motive, not merely as the occasion or condition of volition, but as that which *produces* it. This position, as we have seen, has been denied by high authority; and therefore it becomes necessary to establish it, in order that I may not be charged with disputing only about words; and that although I may be exceedingly "desirous of being thought to differ with President Edwards" on this subject, yet I do "most exactly agree with him."

To begin then;—if motive is merely the condition on which the mind acts, and exerts no influence in the production of volition, it is certainly improper to say, that it *gives rise to volition*. This clearly implies that it is the efficient, or producing cause of volition. On this point, let the younger Edwards himself be the judge. "That self-determination *gives rise* to volition," is an expression which he quotes from Dr. Chauncey, and italicizes the words "gives rise to," as showing that the author of them regarded the mind as the efficient cause of volition. Now, President Edwards says, that the "strongest motive excites the mind to volition;" and he adds, that "the notion of exciting, is *exerting influence to cause the effect to arise and come forth into existence*," p. 96. Surely, if to give rise to a thing, is efficiently to cause it, no less can be said of exerting influence "to *cause it to arise and come forth into existence*." And if so, then, according to the younger Edwards himself, the author of the Inquiry regarded motive as the efficient cause of volition; and yet, on p. 66 he declares, that President Edwards did not hold "motive to be the efficient cause of volition;" and that if he has dropped any expression which implies such a doctrine, it must have been an inadvertency. I intend to show, before I have done, that there are many such inadvertencies in his work; the younger Edwards himself being the judge.

Now, it will not be denied, that that which produces a thing, is its efficient cause. The younger Edwards himself has spoken of an "*efficient, producing cause*," in such a manner as to show that he regarded them as convertible terms, p. 46. He being judge, then, that which produces a thing, is its efficient cause. I might easily show, if it were necessary, that he himself frequently speaks of motive as the efficient, or producing cause of volition; but, at present, I am only concerned with the doctrine of President Edwards. "It is true," says President Edwards, "I find myself possessed of my volitions before I can see the effectual power of any cause to *produce* them, for the power and *efficacy* of the cause is not seen but by the effect," p. 277. Here, from the volition, from the effect, he infers the operation of the cause or power which *produces* it. Now this cause is motive, the strongest motive; for this is that which operates to induce a choice. Motive, then, *produces* volition, according to the Inquiry; it is not merely the condition on which it is produced.

The younger Edwards declares, that President Edwards did not regard "motive as the efficient cause of volition," p. 66, but only as the "occasion or previous circumstances necessary to volition;" in this respect "most exactly agreeing with Dr. West" himself; and yet he tells us, in another place, that "every cause of volition is included in President Edwards' definition of motive," p. 104. Now, does not every cause of volition include the efficient cause thereof? Does not this expression include that which is the cause of volition in the real, in the only proper, sense of the word?

To save the consistency of the author, will it be said, that "every cause" does not include the efficient cause in his estimation, since in his opinion there is no such cause? If this should be said, it would not be true; for the younger Edwards did, as it is well known, regard the influence of the Divine Being as the efficient cause of volition. He regarded the Deity as the sole fountain of all efficiency in heaven and in earth. Hence, if the definition of President Edwards included "every cause" of volition; it must have included this divine influence, this efficient cause. Indeed, the younger Edwards expressly asserts, that this "divine influence" is included in President Edwards' "explanation of his idea of motive," p. 104. He tells us, then, that President Edwards regards motive as merely the *occasion* of volition; and yet

14

that he considered motive as including the efficient cause of volition! At one time, motive is merely the antecedent, which exerts no influence; at another, it embraces the efficient cause! At one time, the author of the Inquiry "most exactly agrees" with the libertarian in regard to this all-important point; and, at another, he most perfectly disagrees with him! It is to be hoped, that President Edwards is not quite so glaringly inconsistent with himself, on this subject, as he is represented to be by his distinguished son.

Again. President Edwards has written a section to prove, that "volitions are necessarily connected with the influence of motives;" which clearly implies that they are brought to pass by the influence of motives. In this section, he says, "Motives do nothing, as motives or inducements, but by their influence. And so much as is *done by their influence* is the effect of them. For that is the notion of an effect, something that *is brought to pass* by the influence of something else." Here motives are said to be the causes of volitions, and to *bring them to pass by their influence*. Is this to make motive merely the condition on which the mind acts? Is this to consider it as merely an antecedent to volition, which exerts no influence? On the contrary, does it not strongly remind one of that "restrained sense of the word cause," in which it signifies, that which "has an influence to produce a thing, *or bring it to pass?*"

Once more. In relation to the acts of the will, he adopts the following language to show that they are necessarily dependent on the influence of motives: "For an event to have a cause and ground of its existence, and yet not be connected with its cause, is an inconsistency. For if the event be not connected with the cause, it is not dependent on its cause; its *existence* is as it were *loose from its influence*; and it may attend it, or it may not; its being a mere contingency, whether it follows or attends the influence of the cause, or not; and that is the same thing as not to be dependent on it. And to say the event is not dependent on its cause, *is absurd*; it is the same thing as to say, it is not its cause, nor the event the effect of it; for dependence on *the influence of a cause is the very notion of an effect*. If there be no such relation between one thing and another, consisting in the connexion and dependence of one thing on the influence of another, then it is certain there is no such relation between them as is signified by the relation of cause and effect," p. 77-8. Now, here we are told, that it is the very notion of an effect, that it owes its existence to the influence of its cause; and that *it is absurd* to speak of an effect which is loose from the influence of its cause. It is this influence, "which causes volition to arise and come forth into existence." Any other notion of cause and effect is absurd and unmeaning. And yet, President

Edwards informs us, that he sometimes uses the term cause to signify any antecedent, though it may exert no influence; and that he so employs it, in order to prevent cavilling and objecting. Now, what is all this taken together, but to inform us, that he sometimes uses the word in question *very absurdly*, in order to keep us from finding fault with him? The truth is, that whatever apparent concession President Edwards may have made, he does habitually bring down the term *cause* to its narrow and restrained sense, to its strict and proper meaning, when he says, that motive is the cause of volition. He loses sight entirely of the idea, that it is only the *occasion* on which the mind acts.

I might multiply extracts to the same effect almost without end; but it is not necessary. It must be evident to every impartial reader of the Inquiry, that even if the author really meant by the above extracts, that motive is merely the antecedent to volition; this was only a momentary concession made to his opponents, with the vague and ill-defined hope, perhaps, that it would render his system less obnoxious to them. It had no abiding place in his mind. It was no sooner uttered than it was repelled and driven away by the whole tenor of his system. We soon hear him, as if no such thing had ever been dreamed of in his philosophy, asking the question, and that too, in relation to motives, "What *can be meant by a cause*, but something that is the ground and reason of a thing *by its influence*, AN INFLUENCE THAT IS PREVALENT AND EFFECTUAL," p. 97. Will it be pretended, that this does not come up to his definition of an efficient cause, as that which brings something to pass by "a *positive* influence?" Such a pretext would amount to nothing; for Edwards has said, that "motives excite volition;" and "to excite, *is to be a cause in the most proper sense, not merely a negative occasion, but a ground of existence by positive influence*," p. 96.

An efficient cause is properly defined by the Edwardses themselves. "Does not the man talk absurdly and inconsistently," says the younger Edwards, "who asserts, that a man is the efficient cause of his own volitions, yet puts forth no exertion in order to cause it? If any other way of *efficiently* causing an effect, be possible or conceivable, let it be pointed out," p.49. President Edwards evidently entertained the same idea; for he repeatedly says, that if the mind be the cause of its own volitions, it must cause them by a preceding act of the mind. The objection which he urges against the self-determining power, is founded on this idea of a cause. It is what he means, when he says, that the term *cause* is "often used in so restrained a sense as to signify only that which has a *positive efficiency* or *influence* to *produce* a thing, or *bring it to pass*."

That President Edwards regarded motive as the efficient or producing cause of volition, according to his own notion of it, is clear not only from numerous passages of the Inquiry; it is also wrought into the very substance and structure of his whole argument. It is involved in his very definition of the strongest motive. The strongest motive, says he, is the whole of that which "*operates* to induce a particular choice." Now, to say that one thing *operates* to induce another, or bring it into existence, is, according to the definition of the younger Edwards himself, to say that it is the efficient cause of the thing so produced. If there be any meaning in words, or any truth in the definition of the Edwardses, then to say that one thing operates to produce another, is to say that it is its efficient cause. President Edwards, as we have seen, holds that motive is "the effectual power and efficacy" which produces volition.

Again. Edwards frequently says, that "if this great principle of common sense, that every effect must have a cause, be given up, then there will be no such thing as reasoning from effect to cause. We cannot even prove the existence of Deity. If any thing can begin to be without a cause of its existence, then we cannot know that there is a God." Now, the sense in which this maxim is here used is perfectly obvious; for nothing can begin to be without an efficient cause, by which it is brought into existence. When we reason from those things which begin to be up to God, we clearly reason from effects to their efficient causes. Hence, when this maxim is applied by Edwards to volitions, he evidently refers to the efficient causes of them. If he does not, his maxim is misapplied; for it is established in one sense, and applied in another. If it proves any thing, it proves that volition must have an efficient cause; and when motive is taken to be that cause, it is taken to be the efficient cause of volition.

This is not all. Edwards undertakes to point out the difference between natural and moral necessity. In the case of moral necessity, says he, "the cause with which the effect is connected is of a particular kind: viz., that which is of a moral nature; either some previous habitual disposition, or some motive presented to the understanding. And the effect is also of a particular kind, being likewise of a moral nature; consisting in some inclination or volition of the soul, or voluntary action." But the difference, says he, "does not lie so much *in the nature of the connection*, as in the two terms connected." Now, let us suppose that any effect, the creation of the world, for example, is produced by the power of God. In this case, the connection between the effect produced, the creation of the world, and the act of the divine omnipotence by which it is created, is certainly the connection between an effect and its efficient cause. The two terms are here connected by a natural necessity. But we are most explicitly informed, that the connection between motives and volitions, differs from this in the nature of the two terms connected, rather than in the nature of the connection. How could language more clearly or precisely convey the meaning of an author? To say that President Edwards does not make motive the efficient cause of volition, is, indeed, not so much to interpret, as it is to new model, his philosophy of the will.

The connection between the strongest motive, he declares, and the corresponding volition, is "absolute," just as absolute as any connection in the world. If the strongest motive exists, the volition is sure to follow; it necessarily follows; it is *absurd* to suppose, that it may attend its cause or not. To say that it may follow the influence of its cause, or may not, is to say that it is not dependent on that influence, that it is not the effect of it. In other words, it is to say that a volition is the effect of the strongest motive, and yet that it is not the effect of it; which is a plain contradiction. Such, as we have seen, is the clear and unequivocal teaching of the Inquiry.

In conclusion, if Edwards really held, that motive does not produce volition, but is merely the occasion on which it is put forth, where shall we find his doctrine? Where shall we look for it? We hear him charged with destroying man's free-agency, by making motive the producing cause of volition; and we see him labouring to repel this charge. Truly, if he held the doctrine ascribed to him, we might have expected to find some allusion to it in his attempts to refute such a charge. If such had been his doctrine, with what ease might he have repelled the charge in question, and shown its utter futility, by simply alleging that, according to his system, motive is the occasion, and not the producing cause, of volition? Instead of the many pages through which he has so laboriously struggled, in order to bring our ideas of free-agency and virtue into harmony with his scheme; with what infinite ease might a single word have brought his scheme into harmony with the common sentiments of mankind in regard to free-agency and virtue! Indeed, if Edwards really believed that motive is merely the condition on which the mind acts, nothing can be more wonderful than his profound silence in regard to it on such an occasion; except the great pains which, on all occasions, he has taken to keep it entirely in the background. If the younger Edwards is not mistaken as to the true import of his father's doctrine, then, instead of setting it forth in a clear light, so that it may be read of all men, the author of the Inquiry has, indeed, enveloped it in such a flood of darkness, that it is no wonder those who have been so fortunate as to find it out, should be so frequently called upon to complain that his opponents do not understand him. Indeed, if such be the doctrine of the Inquiry, I do not see how any man can possibly understand it, unless he has inherited some peculiar power, unknown to the rest of mankind, by which its occult meaning may be discerned, notwithstanding all the outward appearances by which it is contradicted and obscured.

The plain truth is, as we have seen, that President Edwards holds motive to be the producing cause of volition. According to his scheme, "Volitions are necessarily connected with the influence of motives;" they "are brought to pass by the prevailing and effectual influence" of motives. Motive is "the effectual power and efficacy" by which they are "produced." They are not merely caused to be thus, and not otherwise, by motive; they are "caused to arise and come forth into existence." This is the great doctrine for which Edwards contends; and this is precisely the doctrine which I deny. *I contend against no other kind of necessity but this moral necessity, just as it is explained by Edwards himself.*

Here the issue with President Edwards is joined; and I intend to hold him steadily to it. No ambiguity of words shall, for a moment, divert my mind from it. If his arguments, when thoroughly sifted and scrutinized, establish this doctrine; then shall I lay down my arms and surrender at discretion. But if his assumptions are unsound, or his deductions false, I shall hold them for naught. If he reconciles his scheme of moral necessity with the reality of virtue, with the moral agency and accountability of man, and with the purity of God; then I shall lay aside my objections; but if, in reality, he only reconciles it with the semblance of these things, whilst he denies their substance, I shall not be diverted from an opposition to so monstrous a system, by the fair appearances it may be made to wear to the outward eye.

SECTION III.

THE great doctrine of the Inquiry seems to go round in a vicious circle, to run into an insignificant truism. This is a grave charge, I am aware, and I have ventured to make it only after the most mature reflection: and the justness of it, may be shown by a variety of considerations.

In the first place, when we ask, "what determines the will?" the author replies, "it is the strongest motive;" and yet, according to his definition, the strongest motive is that which determines the will. Thus, says Edwards, "when I speak of the strongest motive, I have respect to the whole that operates to induce a particular act of volition, whether that be the strength of one thing alone, or of many together." If we ask, then, what produces any particular act of volition, we are told, it is the strongest motive; and if we inquire what is the strongest motive, we are informed, it is the whole of that which operated to produce that particular act of volition. What is this but to inform us, that an act of volition is produced by that which produces it?

It is taken for granted by President Edwards, that volition is an effect, and consequently has a cause. The great question, according to his work, is, what is this cause? He says it is the strongest motive; in the definition of which he includes every thing that in any way contributes to the production of volition; in other words, the strongest motive is made to embrace every thing that acts as a cause of volition. This is the way in which he explains himself, as well as the manner in which he is understood by others. Thus, says the younger Edwards, "in his explanation of his idea of motive, he mentions all agreeable objects and views, all reasons and arguments, and all internal biases and tempers, which have a tendency to volition; i. e. every *cause* or *occasion* of volition," p. 104. Every reader of President Edwards must be satisfied that this is a correct account of his definition of motive; and this being the case, the whole amounts to just this proposition, that volition is caused by that which causes it! He admits that it would be hard, if not impossible, to enumerate all those things and circumstances which aid in the production of volition; but still he is quite sure, that the whole of that which operates to produce a volition does actually produce it! Though he may have failed to show wherein consists the strength of motives; yet he contends that the strongest motive, or the cause of volition, is really and unquestionably the cause of volition! Such is the great doctrine of the Inquiry.

If this is what the Inquiry means to establish, surely it rests upon unassailable ground. Well may President Day assert, that "to say a weaker motive prevails against a stronger one is to say, that that which has the least influence has the greatest influence," p. 66. Now who would deny this position of the learned president? Who would say, that that which has the greatest influence has not the greatest influence? Surely, this great doctrine is to the full as certain as the newly discovered axiom of professor Villant, that "a thing is equal to itself!"

President Day, following in the footsteps of Edwards, informs us that the will is determined by the strongest motive; but how shall we know what is the strongest motive? "The strength of a motive," says he, "is not its prevailing, but the power by which it prevails. Yet we may very properly measure *this power by the actual result!*" Thus are we gravely informed that the will is determined by that which determines it.

Again. If we suppose there is a real strength in motives, that they exert a positive influence in the production of volitions, then we concede every thing to President Edwards. For, if motives are so many forces acting upon the will, to say that the strongest will prevail, is simply to say that it is the strongest. But if motives exert no positive influence, then when we say that one is stronger than another, we must be understood to use this expression in a metaphorical sense; we must refer to some property of motives which we figuratively call their strength, and of which we suppose one motive to possess a greater degree than another. If this be so, what is this common property of motives, which we call their strength? If they do not possess a real strength, if they do not exert an efficient influence; but are merely said, metaphorically speaking, to possess such power and to exert such influence; then what becomes of the self-evidence which President Edwards claims for his fundamental proposition motives exert a real force, of course the strongest must prevail; but if they only have something else about them, which we call their strength, it is not self-evident that the motive which possesses this something else in the highest degree must necessarily prevail. Hence, the great doctrine of President Edwards is either a proposition whose truth arises out of the very definition of the terms in which it is expressed, or it is utterly destitute of that axiomatical certainty which he claims for it. In other words, he has settled his great doctrine of the will by the mere force of a definition; or he has left its foundations quite unsettled.

Motives, as they are called, are different from each other in nature and in kind; and hence, it were absurd to compare them in degree. "The strongest motive," therefore, is a mode of expression which can have no intelligible meaning, unless it be used with reference to the influence which motives are supposed to exert over the mind. This is the sense in which it clearly seems to be used by Edwards. The distinguishing property of a motive, according to his definition, is nothing in the nature of the motive itself; it consists in its adaptedness "to move or excite the mind to volition;" nor indeed could he find any other way of measuring or determining what he calls the strength of motives, since they are so diverse in their own nature from each other. He could not have given any plausible definition of the strength of motives, if he had looked at them as they are in themselves; and hence, he was under the necessity of defining it, by a reference to the "degree of tendency or *advantage* they have to move or excite the will." Thus, according to the Inquiry, the will is determined by the strongest motive; and yet we can form no intelligible idea of what is meant by the strongest motive, unless we conceive it to be that which determines the will. The matter will not be mended, by alleging that the strongest motive is not defined to be that which actually determines the will, but that which has the greatest degree of previous tendency or advantage, to excite or move it; for we cannot know what motive has this greatest degree of previous tendency or advantage, except by observing what motive actually does determine the will.

This leads us to another view of the same subject. The strength of a motive, as President Edwards properly remarks, depends upon the state of the mind to which it is addressed. Hence, in a great majority of cases, we can know nothing about the relative strength of motives, except from the actual influence which they exert over the mind of the individual upon whom they are brought to bear. This shows that the universal proposition, that the will is *always* determined by the strongest motive, can be known to be true, only by assuming that the strongest motive is that by which the will is determined.

The same thing may be made to appear from another point of view. It has been well said by the philosopher of Malmsbury, "that experience concludeth nothing universally." From experience we can pronounce, only in so far as we have observed, and no farther. But the proposition, that the will is always determined by the strongest motive, is a universal proposition; and hence, if true at all, its truth could not have been learnt from observation and experience. It must depend upon the very definition of the terms in which it is expressed. We cannot say that the will is in all cases determined by the strongest motive, unless we include in the very idea and definition of the strongest motive, that it is such that it determines the will. President Edwards not only does, but he must necessarily, go around in this circle, in order to give any degree of clearness and certainty to his doctrine.

That President Edwards goes around in this vicious circle, may be shown in another way. "It appears from these things," says he, "that in some sense, *the will always follows the last dictate of the understanding.* But then the *understanding* must be taken in a large sense, as including the whole faculty of perception or apprehension, and not merely what is called reason or judgment. If by the last dictate of the understanding is meant what reason declares to be best, or most for the person's happiness, taking in the whole of its duration, it is not true, that the will always follows the last dictate of the understanding," p. 25. In this place, President Edwards gives no distinct idea of what he means by the last dictate of the understanding, which the will is said to follow in all cases. But in the eighth volume of his works, that dictate of the understanding which the will is said to follow, is called the "practical judgment;" and this is defined to be, "that judgment which men make of things that prevail, so as to determine their actions and govern their practice." Here again are we informed, that the will always follows the practical judgment, and that the practical judgment is that which men make of things that prevail, so as to determine the will.

The Inquiry itself furnishes abundant evidence, that I have done its author no injustice. "I have chosen," says he, "rather to express myself thus, *that the will always is as the greatest apparent good, or as what appears most agreeable*, than to say the will is determined by the greatest apparent good, or by what seems most agreeable; because an appearing most agreeable to the mind, and the mind's preferring, seem scarcely distinct. If strict propriety of speech be insisted on, it may more properly be said, that the *voluntary action*, which is the immediate consequence of the mind's choice, is determined by that which appears most agreeable, than the choice itself." After all, then, it seems that choice itself, or volition, is not determined by that which appears the most agreeable; because, in reality, the sense of the most agreeable and volition are one and the same thing. But surely, if we cannot distinguish between choice and the sense of the most agreeable, then to say that the one always is as the other, is only to say that a thing is always as it is. Edwards saw the absurdity of saying that a thing is determined by itself; but he does not seem to have seen how insignificant is the proposition, that a thing is always as it is, and not otherwise; and hence this is the form in which he has chosen to present the great leading idea of his work on the will. And henceforth we are to understand, that the preference of the mind is always as that which appears most agreeable to the mind; or, in other words, that the preference or choice of the mind is always as the choice of the mind.

This is not all. President Edwards himself has frequently reduced the fundamental doctrine of the Inquiry to an identical proposition. It is well known, that "to be determined by the strongest motive," "to follow the greatest apparent good," "to do what is most agreeable," or "what pleases most," are all different modes of expression employed by him to set forth the same fundamental doctrine. In speaking of this doctrine, he says: "There is scarcely a plainer and more *universal* dictate of the sense and experience of mankind, than that, when men act voluntarily, and do what they please, then they do what suits them best, or what is most *agreeable to them*. To say, that they do what *pleases* them, but yet not what is agreeable to them, is the same thing as to say, they do what they please, but do not act their pleasure; and that is to say, that they do what they please, and yet do not what they please." Most assuredly, if to deny the leading proposition of the Inquiry, is to deny that men do what they please when they do what they please; then to affirm it, is only to advance the insignificant truism, that men do what they please when they do what they please. It seems to me, that after President Edwards had reduced his fundamental proposition to such a truism, he might very well have spared himself the three hundred pages that follow.

Again, he says: "It is manifest that no acts of the will are contingent, in such sense as to be without all necessity, or so as not to be necessary with a necessity of consequence and connection; because every act of the will is some way connected with the understanding, and is as the greatest apparent good is, in the manner which has already been explained; namely, that the soul always wills or chooses that, which in the present view of the mind, considered in the whole of that view, and all that belongs to it, appears most agreeable. Because, as we observed before, nothing is more evident than that, when men act voluntarily, and do what they please, then they do what appears most agreeable to them; and to say otherwise would be as much as to affirm, that men do not choose what appears to suit them best, or what seems most pleasing to them; or that they do not choose what they prefer, *which brings the matter to a contradiction.*"

Thus, the great fundamental doctrine of the Inquiry is reduced by Edwards himself to the barren truism, that men do actually choose what they choose; a proposition which the boldest advocate of free-agency would hardly dare to call in question. After labouring through a whole section to establish this position, the author concludes by saying, "These things may serve, I hope, in some measure to illustrate and confirm the position laid down in the beginning of this section: viz. That the will is always determined by the strongest motive, or by the view of the mind which has the greatest previous tendency to excite volition. But whether I have been so happy as rightly to explain the thing wherein consists the strength of motives, or not, *yet my failing in this will not overthrow the position itself; which carries much of its own evidence along with it, and is a point of chief importance to the purpose of the ensuing discourse:* and the truth of it I hope will appear *with great clearness*, before I have finished what I have to say on the subject of human liberty." Truly the position in question, as it is explained by the author himself, carries not only much, but all, of its own evidence along with it. Who can deny that a man always does what he pleases, when he does what he pleases? This truth appears with just as great clearness at the beginning, as it does at the conclusion, of the celebrated Inquiry of the author. It is invested in a flood of light, which can neither be increased by argument, nor obscured by sophistry.

From the foregoing remarks, it appears, I think, that the fundamental doctrine of the Inquiry is a barren truism, or a vicious circle. If Edwards understood the import of his own doctrine, when he reduced it to the form that a man does what he pleases when he does what he pleases, it is certainly a truism; and if this is all his famous doctrine amounts to, it can have no bearing whatever upon the question as to the cause of volition; for whether the mind be the cause of its own volitions, or whether the strongest motive always causes them, or whether they have no causes at all, it is equally and unalterably true, that every man does what he pleases when he does what he pleases. There is no possible form of the doctrine of free-agency or contingency, however wild, which is at all inconsistent with such a truism.

Edwards is not always consistent with himself. He sometimes represents the greatest apparent good, or sense of the most agreeable, as the cause of volition; and then his doctrine assumes the form, that the will is determined by the strongest motive, or the greatest apparent good. And yet he sometimes identifies a sense of the most agreeable with the choice itself; and then his doctrine assumes the form that the choice of the mind is always as the choice of the mind; and to deny it is a plain contradiction in terms.

From the fact that Edwards has gone round in a circle, it has been concluded that he has begged the question; but how, or wherein he has begged it, is a point which has not been sufficiently noticed. The very authors who have uttered this complaint, have granted him the very thing for which he has begged. If volition is an *effect*, if it has a *cause*, then most unquestionably the cause of volition is the cause of volition. Admit that volition is an effect, as so many libertarians have done, and then his definition of motive, which includes every cause of volition, places his doctrine upon an immutable foundation. We might as well heave at the everlasting mountains as to try to shake it.

Admit that volition is an effect, and what can we say? Can we say, that the strongest motive may exist, and yet no volition may follow from it? To this the necessitarian would instantly reply, that it any thing exists, and no volition follows thereupon, it is evidently not the cause of volition, and consequently is not the strongest motive; for this, according to the definition, includes every cause of volition: it is indeed absurd, to suppose that an effect should not proceed from its cause: This is the ground taken both by President Edwards and President Day. It is absurd, says the latter, to suppose that a weaker motive, or any thing else, can prevail over the stronger—and why? Because the strongest motive is that which prevails. "If it be said," he continues, "that *something else* gives the weaker motive a superiority over the stronger; *then this something else is itself a motive*, and the united influence of the two is greater than that of the third," p. 66. Thus, say what we will, we can never escape this admirable net of words, that the will is determined by that which determines it.

I do not intend, then, to engage in the hopeless task, of admitting volition to be an effect, and yet striving to extricate it from "the mechanism of cause and effect." This ground has long since been occupied by much abler persons than myself; and if they have failed of success, falling into innumerable inconsistencies, it is because, on such ground, success is impossible; and that notwithstanding their transcendant abilities, they have been fated to contradict themselves.

SECTION IV.

VOLITION NOT AN EFFECT.

THE argument of the Inquiry, as I have shown, assumes that a volition is an effect in the proper sense of the word; that it is the correlative of an efficient cause. If it were necessary, this point might be established by a great variety of additional considerations; but, I presume that every candid reader of the Inquiry is fully satisfied in relation to it.

If we mean by an effect, every thing that comes to pass, of course a volition is an effect; for no one can deny that it comes to pass. Or, if we include in the definition of the term, every thing which has a sufficient reason and ground of its existence, we cannot deny that it embraces the idea of a volition. For, under certain circumstances, the free mind will furnish a sufficient reason and ground of the existence of a volition. All that I deny is, that a volition does proceed from the mind, or from motive, or from anything else, in the same manner that an effect, properly so called, proceeds from its efficient cause.

This is a point on which I desire to be distinctly understood. I put forth a volition to move my hand. The motion of the hand follows. Now, here I observe the action of the mind, and also the motion of the hand. The effect exists in the body, in that which is by nature passive; the cause in that which is active, in the mind. The effect produced in the body, in the hand, is the passive result of the prior direct action of the mind. It is in this restricted sense, that I use the term in question, when I deny that a volition is an effect. I do not deny that it depends for its production upon certain circumstances, as the conditions of action, and upon the powers of the mind, by which it is capable of acting in view of such circumstances. All that I deny is, that volition results from the prior action of mind, or of circumstances, or of any thing else, in the same manner that the motion of body results from the prior action of mind. Or, in other words, I contend that action is the invariable antecedent of bodily motion, but not of volition; that whatever may be its relations to other things, a volition does not sustain the same relation to any thing in the universe, that an effect sustains to its efficient cause, that a passive result sustains to the direct prior action by which it is produced. I hope I may be *always* so understood, when I affirm that a volition is not an effect.

It is in this narrow and restricted sense that Edwards assumes a volition to be an effect. He does not say, in so many words, that the mind cannot put forth a volition, except in the way of producing it by a preceding volition or act of the will; but he first assumes a volition to be an effect; and then he asserts, that the mind can be the cause of no *effect*, (italicising the term effect,) except by the prior action of the mind. Thus, having assumed a volition to be an effect, he takes it for granted that it cannot proceed from the mind in any way, except that in which any effect in the outer world proceeds from the mind; that is to say, except it be produced by the direct prior action of the mind, by a preceding volition. Thus he brings the idea of a volition under the above narrow and restricted notion of an effect; and thereby confounds the relation which subsists between mind and its volitions, with the relation which subsists between mind and its external effects in body. In other words, on the supposition that our volitions proceed from the mind, he takes it for granted that they must be produced by the preceding action of the mind; just as an effect, in the limited sense of the term, is produced by the prior action of its cause. It is in this assumption, that Edwards lays the foundation of the logic, by which he reduces the self-determining power of the mind to the absurdity of an infinite series of volitions.

It is evident that such is the course pursued by Edwards; for he not only calls a volition, an effect, but he also says, that the mind can "bring no *effects* to pass, but what are consequent upon its acting," p. 56. And again he says, "The will determines which way the hands and feet shall move, by an act of choice; and *there is no other way* of the will's determining, directing, or commanding any thing at all." This is very true, if a volition is such an effect as requires the prior action of something else to account for its production, just as the motion of the "hands and feet" requires the action of the mind to account for its production; but it is not true, if a volition is such an effect, that its existence may be accounted for by the presence of certain circumstances or motives, as the conditions of action, in conjunction with a mind capable of acting in view of such motives. In other words, his assertion is true, if we allow him to assume, as he does, that a volition is an effect, in the above restricted meaning of the term; but it is not true, if we consider a volition as an effect in a larger sense of the word. Hence, the whole strength of Edwards' position lies in the sense which he arbitrarily attaches to the term *effect*, when he says that a volition is an effect.

Now, is a volition an effect in such a sense of the word? Is it brought into existence, like the motion of body, by the prior action of any thing else? We answer, No. But how shall this point be decided? The necessitarian says, a moment before the volition did not exist, now it does exist; and hence, it necessarily follows, that there must have been a cause by which it was brought into existence. That is to say, it *must* be an effect. True, it must be an effect, if you please; but in what sense of the word? Is volition an effect, in the same sense that the motion of the body is an effect? This is the question.

And this question, I contend, is not to be decided by abstract considerations, nor yet by the laying of words together, and drawing conclusions from them. It is a question, not of logic, but of psychology. By whatever name you may please to call it, the true nature of a volition is not to be determined by reference to abstractions, nor by the power of words; but *by simply looking at it and seeing what it is.* If we would really understand its nature, we must not undertake to *reason it out;* we must *open our eyes*, and *look*, and *see*. The former course would do very well, no doubt, if the object were to construct a world for ourselves; but if we would behold the glory of that which God has constructed for us, and in us, we must lay aside the proud syllogistic method of the schools, and betake ourselves to the humble task of observation—of patient, severe, and scrutinizing observation. There is no other condition on which we can "enter into the kingdom of man, which is founded in the sciences." There is no other course marked out for us by the immortal Bacon: and if we pursue any other we may wander in the dazzling light of a thousand abstractions, and behold whatever fleeting images of grandeur and of beauty we may be pleased to conjure up for ourselves; but the pure light of nature and of truth will be hid from us.

What then is a volition just as it is revealed to us in the light of consciousness? Does it result from the prior action of mind, or of motive, or of any thing else? In other words, is it an *effect*, as the motion of body is an effect!

We always conceive of the subject in which such an effect resides, as being wholly passive. President Edwards himself has repeatedly said, that it is the very notion of an effect, that it results from the action or influence of its cause; and that nothing is any further an effect, than as it proceeds from that action or influence. The subject in which it is produced, is always passive as to its production; and just in so far as it is itself active, it is not the subject of an effect, but the author of an action. Such is the idea of an effect in the true and proper sense of the word.

Now does our idea of a volition correspond with this idea of an effect? Is it produced in the mind, and is the mind passive as to its production? Is it, like the motion of a body, the passive result of the action of something else? No. It is not the result of action; it is action itself. The mind is not passive as to its production; it is in and of itself an action of the mind. It is not *determined*; it is a *determination*. It is not a produced effect, like the motion of body; it is itself an original producing cause. It does seem to me, that if any man will only reflect on this subject, he must see that there is a clear and manifest difference between an ACT and an EFFECT.

Although the scheme of Edwards identifies these two things, and his argument assumes them to be one and the same; yet his language, it appears to me, frequently betrays the fact, that his consciousness did not work in harmony with his theory. While speaking of the acts of the will as effects, he frequently says, that it is the very idea of an effect that it results from, and is necessarily connected with, the action of its cause, and that it is absurd to suppose that it is free or loose from the influence of its cause.

And yet, in reference to volitions, he often uses the expression, *"this sort of effects,"* as if it did not exactly correspond with the "very idea of an effect," from which it is absurd to depart in our conceptions. When he gives fair play to consciousness, he speaks of different kinds of effects; and yet, when he returns to his theory and his reasoning, all this seems to vanish; and there remains but one clear, fixed, and definite idea of an effect, and to speak of any thing else as such is absurd. He now and then pays a passing tribute to the power of consciousness, by admitting that the soul exerts its own volitions, that the soul itself acts; but he no sooner comes to the work of argument and refutation, than it is motive that "causes them to be put forth or exerted," p. 96. Ever and anon, he seems to catch a whisper from the voice of consciousness; and he concedes that he sometimes uses the term cause to designate that which has not a *positive* or *productive* influence, p. 50-1. But this is not when he is engaged in the energy of debate. Let Mr. Chubb cross his path; let him hear the voice of opposition giving utterance to the sentiment, that "in motive there is no causality in the production of action;" and that moment the voice of consciousness is hushed in the most profound silence. He rises, like a giant, in the defence of his system, and he declares, that "to excite," as motives do, "is positively to do something," and "certainly that which does something, is the cause of the thing done by it." Yea, "to excite, *is to cause in the most proper sense, not merely a negative occasion*, but a ground of existence by *positive influence*," p. 96.

These passages, which are scattered up and down through the Inquiry, in which the doctrine of liberty seems to be conceded, I cannot but regard as highly important concessions. They have been used to show that we misconceive the scheme of Edwards, when we ascribe to him the doctrine of fate. But when they are thus adduced, to show that we misrepresent his doctrine, I beg it may be remembered that such evidence can prove only one of two things; either that we do not understand what he teaches, or that he is not always consistent with himself.

If he really held the doctrine of fatalism, we ought not to be surprised that he has furnished such evidence against himself. It is not in the nature of the human mind to keep itself always deaf to the voice of consciousness. It is not in the power of any system always to counteract the spontaneous workings of nature. Though the mind should be surrounded by those deep-seated, all-pervading, and obstinate illusions, by which the scheme of fatalism is made to wear the appearance of self-evident truth; yet when it loses sight of that system, it will, at times, speak out in accordance with the dictates of nature. The stern and unrelenting features of fatalism cannot always be so intimately present to the mind, as entirely to exclude it from the contemplation of a milder and more captivating system of philosophy. Notwithstanding the influence of system, how rigid soever may be its demands, the human mind will, in its moments of relaxation, recognize *in its feelings* and *in its utterance*, those great truths which are inseparable from its very nature.

Let it be borne in mind, then, that there is more than one process in the universe. Some things are produced, it is most true, by the prior action of other things; and herein we behold the relation of cause and effect, properly so called; but it does not follow, that all things are embraced by this *one* relation. This appears to be so only to the mind of the necessitarian; from which one fixed idea has shut out the light of observation. He no longer sees the rich variety, the boundless diversity, there is in the works of God: all things and all modes and all processes of the awe-inspiring universe, are made to conform to the narrow and contracted methods of his own mind. Look where he will, he sees not the "free and flowing outline" of nature's true lineaments; he every where beholds the image of the one fixed idea in his mind, projected outwardly upon the universe of God; behind which the true secrets and operations of nature are concealed from his vision. Even when he contemplates that living source of action, that bubbling fountain of volitions, the immortal mind of man itself, he only beholds a *thing*, which is made to act by the action of something else upon it; just as a body is made to move by the action of force upon it. His philosophy is, therefore, an essentially shallow and superficial philosophy. The great name of Edwards cannot shield it from such condemnation.

SECTION V.

OF THE CONSEQUENCES OF REGARDING VOLITION AS AN EFFECT.

IT has been frequently conceded that a volition is an effect; but to make this concession, without explanation or qualification, is to surrender the whole cause of free agency into the hand of the enemy. For if a volition is an effect, properly speaking, the only question is as to its efficient cause: it is necessarily produced by its cause.

To make this matter clear, let us consider what is precisely meant by the term cause when it is thus used? An effect is necessarily connected, not with the *thing* which is sometimes called its cause, but with the *action* or *positive influence* of that thing. Thus, the mind, or the power of the mind, is sometimes said to be the cause of motion in the body; but this is not to speak with philosophical precision. No motion of the body is necessarily connected, either with the mind itself, or with the power of the mind. In other words, if these should lie dormant, or fail to act, they would produce no bodily motion. But let the mind act, or will a particular motion, and the body will necessarily move in consequence of that action. Hence, it is neither with the mind, nor with the power of the mind, that bodily motion, as an effect, is necessarily connected; it is with an act of the mind or volition that this necessary connection subsists. A cause is said to imply its effect: it is not the mind, but an act of the mind, that implies motion in the body.

This is evidently the idea of Edwards, when he says, as he frequently does, that an effect is necessarily connected with the *influence* or *action* of its cause. The term *cause* is ambiguous; and when he says, that an effect is necessarily connected with its cause, he should be understood to mean, in accordance with his own doctrine, that the cause referred to *is the influence* or *action* by which it is produced, and not the thing which exerts that *influence* or *action*. Thus, although motives are said to be causes of action, he contends, they can do nothing except by their influence; and so much as results from their influence is the effect of that influence, and is necessarily connected with it.

Now, if a volition is an effect, if it has an efficient cause, what is that cause? By the *action* of what is it produced? It cannot be by the act of the mind, says Edwards, because the mind can produce an *effect* only by another act. Thus, on the supposition in question, we cannot ascribe a volition to the mind as its cause, without being compelled to admit that it results from a preceding act of the mind. But that preceding act, on the same supposition, will require still another preceding act to account for its production; and so on *ad infinitum.* Such is the absurdity which Edwards delighted to urge against the self-determining power of the mind. It is triumphantly based on the concession that a volition is an effect; that as such the prior *action* of something else is necessary to account for its existence. And if we suppose, in accordance with the truth, that a volition is merely a state of the mind, which does not sustain the same relation to the mind that an effect does to its efficient cause, this absurdity will vanish. The doctrine of liberty will no longer be encumbered with it.

Now, proceeding on the same supposition, let us conceive of a volition as resulting from the influence exerted by motive. If an *act* of the mind is an effect, surely we may say, that the act or productive influence of motive, or of any thing else, is likewise an effect; and consequently must have a cause to account for its existence; and so on *ad infinitum.* Hence, the very absurdity which Edwards charges upon our system, really attaches to his own.

Will it be said that this *ad infinitum* absurdity does not result from the supposition in question, but from the fact that the mind can do nothing except by its action or influence? It is very true, as Edwards repeatedly declares, that the mind can be the cause of no *effect*, except by a preceding act of the mind. The truth of this proposition is involved in the very idea which he attaches to the term *effect*, and it is based upon this idea alone. And we may say, with equal propriety, that motive can be the cause of no *effect*, except by its action or productive influence. Indeed, Edwards himself expressly says, that motives can do nothing, except by an exertion of their influence, or by operating to produce effects. Thus, the two cases are rendered perfectly parallel; and afford the same foundation on which to erect an infinite series of causes.

To evade this, can it be pretended, that motive just exerts this influence of itself? May we not with equal, nay, with infinitely greater propriety, contend that mind just exerts its own positive influence of itself? Or, will it be said, that it is a mistake, to suppose that Edwards ascribed any real, productive, or causal influence to motives; that he regarded them as the *occasions* on which the mind acts, and not properly as the *causes* of its action? If so, then the whole scheme of moral necessity is abandoned, and the doctrine of liberty is left to stand upon its own foundation, in the undisputed evidence of consciousness.

The truth is, if we take it for granted, that a volition is an effect, properly so called, and as such must proceed from the prior action of something else, we cannot escape the *ad infinitum*, absurdity of the Inquiry. If we rise from this platform, we cannot possibly ascend in any direction, without entering upon an infinite series of causes. Whether we ascend through the self-determining power of the mind, or through the determining power of motives, or through the joint action of both, we can save ourselves from such an absurd consequence only by a glaring act of inconsistency. Hence, we are forced back upon the conclusion that action may, and *actually does* arise in the world of mind, without any efficient or producing cause of its existence, without resulting from the prior action of any thing whatever. Any other hypothesis is involved in absurdity.

Let it be assumed, that a volition is, properly speaking, an effect, and every thing is conceded. On this vantage ground, the scheme of necessity may be erected beyond the possibility of an overthrow. For, even if we "suppose that action is determined by the will and free choice," this "is as much as to say, that it must be necessary, being dependent upon, and determined by something foregoing; namely, a foregoing act of choice," p. 199. Let the above position be conceded, and there is no escape from this conclusion. Nay, the conclusion itself is but another mode of stating the position assumed.

It is evident, then, that action must take its rise somewhere in the world, without being caused by prior action; or else there must be an infinite series of acts. I say it takes its rise in the mind, in that which is essentially active, and not in matter. Edwards does not say, that it takes its rise in matter; and hence, there is no dispute on this point. It is very remarkable, that this objection to his scheme, that it runs into an infinite series, seems never to have occurred to President Edwards. He seems to have endeavoured to anticipate and reply to all possible objections to his system; and yet this, which has occurred to so many others, appears not to have occurred to himself, for he has not noticed it.

The younger Edwards has attempted to reply to it. Let us see his reply. "We maintain," says he, "that action may be the effect of a divine influence; or that it may be the effect of one or more second causes, the first of which is immediately produced by the Deity. Here then is not an infinite series of causes, but a very short series, which terminates in the Deity or first cause," p. 121. Thus, according to the younger Edwards, the infinite series of causes is cut short, terminating in the volition of Deity. What! does the volition of God come into existence without a cause of its existence? What then becomes of "that great principle of common sense," so often applied to volition, that no event can begin to be without a cause of its existence? Is this great principle given up? Has it become obsolete?

It may be contended, that although human volition is an effect, and so must have a cause; yet the divine volition is not an effect. The elder Edwards could not have taken this ground; for he contends, that the volition of Deity is just as necessarily connected With the strongest motive, or the greatest apparent good, as is the volition of man. According to the Inquiry, all volitions, both human and divine, are necessarily connected with the greatest apparent good, and in precisely the same manner. The above pretext, therefore, could not have been set up by him.

This ground, however, is taken by the younger Edwards. "It is granted," says he, "that volition in the Deity is not an effect," p. 122; it has no cause, and here terminates the series. But how is this? Can some event, after all, begin to be without having a cause of its existence? without being an effect? By no means. How is it then? Why, says the learned author, the volitions of the Deity have existed from all eternity! They have no causes; because they have never begun to be!

"I deny," says he, "that the operations and energies of the Deity *begin in time*, though the effects of those operations do. They no more begin in time than the divine existence does; but human volitions all begin in time," p. 123. This makes all the difference imaginable; for as the divine acts have existed from all eternity, so they cannot be caused.

But there is an objection to this view. "If it should be said," he continues, "that on this supposition the effects take place not till long after the acts, by which they are produced, I answer, they do so in our view, but not in the view of God. With him there is no time, no before nor after with respect to time," p. 124.

Now, it will not be denied, that things appear to God just as they are in themselves; and hence, if his volitions, which are said to exist long before their effects, even from all eternity, appear to him not to exist long before them; then they do not in reality exist long before them. But if the divine volitions do not really exist long before their effects, but just before them, as other causes do before their effects, why should they not have causes as well as any other volitions? If they really exist just before their effects in time, and not long before them, why do they not exist in time just as much as any other volitions? and why do they not as much require causes to account for their existence? If they only seem to us to exist long before their effects, even from all eternity, how can this mere seeming make any real difference in the case? There is a very short series, we are told, the volition of Deity constituting the first link. Has not this first link, this volition of the Deity, a cause? No. And why? Because it has existed from all eternity; and so nothing could go before it to produce it. Did it not exist long before the effect then, which it produces

35

in time? No. And why? Because in the view of God and in reality, it existed just before its effect, as all causes do, and therefore there is no real severance of cause and effect in the case! It really comes just before its effect in time, and therefore there is no severance of cause and effect; and yet it really existed before all time, even from all eternity, and therefore it cannot have a cause! Now is this logic, or is it legerdemain?

There is no time with God, says the author; then there is no time in reality; it is all an illusion arising from the succession of our own thoughts. If this be so, then all things do really come to pass simultaneously; and if there were a very long series, even an infinite series of causes and effects, yet would they all come to pass in the same instant. Indeed, there is very great uncertainty about the speculations of philosophers in regard to time and space; and we hardly know what to make of them, except we cannot very well understand them; but one thing is abundantly certain; and that is, that it is not good logic, to assert that a particular cause cannot be produced, because it has existed long before its effect, even from all eternity; and yet repel objections to this assertion, by alleging that they only seem to do so, while in reality there is no such tiling. This is to turn from the illusion to the reality, and from the reality to the illusion, just as it suits the exigency of the moment. Such are the poor shifts and shallow devices, to which even gifted minds are reduced, when they refuse to admit that action, that volition, may take its rise in the world, spontaneously proceeding from mind itself, without being made to do so by the action of any thing upon it.

Let us suppose, that a man should tell us, that a producing cause existed long before its effect; that there was nothing to prevent it from bringing its effect to pass; and yet, long after it had existed, its effect sprang up and came into existence; what should we think? Should we not see that it is absurd, in the highest degree, to say that an unimpeded causative act existed yesterday, and even from all eternity, unchanged and unchangeable; and yet its effect did not come to pass until to-day? Surely, no man in his right mind can be made to believe this, unless it be forced upon him by the desperate necessities of a false system; and if any person were told, that although such a thing may seem absurd to us, inasmuch as the cause seems to exist in full operation long before its effect, yet it is not so in the view of God, with whom there is no time, should he not be pardoned if he doubted the infallibility of his informant?

The truth is, we must reason about cause and effect as they appear to us; and whether time be an illusion or not, we must, in all our reasonings, conceive of cause and effect as conjoined in what we call time, or we cannot

36

reason at all. According to the younger Edwards, the act of creation, not the mere purpose to create, but the real causative act of creation, existed in the divine mind from all eternity. Why then did the world spring up and come into existence at one point of time rather than another? How happened it, that so many ages rolled away, and this mighty causative act produced no effect? In view of such a case, how could the author have said, as he frequently does, that a cause necessarily implies its effect? How can this be, if a causative act of the Almighty may exist, and yet, for millions of ages, its omnipotent energy produce no effect? Indeed, such a doctrine destroys all our notions of cause and effect; it overthrows "the great principle of common sense" that cause and effect necessarily imply each other; and involves all our reasoning from cause to effect, and *vice versa*, in the utmost perplexity and confusion. It throws clouds and darkness over the whole field of inquiry.

Since the time of Dr. Samuel Clarke, it has been frequently objected to the scheme of moral necessity, that it is involved in the great absurdity of an infinite series of causes. President Edwards urged this objection against the doctrine of the self-determining power; he did not perceive that it lay against his own scheme of the motive-determining power; and hence, he has not even attempted to answer it. This was reserved for the younger Edwards; and although he has deservedly ranked high as a logician, I cannot but regard his attempt to answer the objection in question, as one of the most remarkable abortions in the history of philosophy.

SECTION VI.

OF THE MAXIM THAT EVERY EFFECT MUST HAVE A CAUSE.

IN a former section, I referred to some of the false assumptions which have been incautiously conceded to the necessitarian, and in which he has laid the foundations of his system; but I have not, as yet, alluded to the argument or deduction in which he is accustomed to triumph. This argument, strange as it may seem, is a deduction, not from any principle or general fact which has been ascertained by observation or experience, but from a self-evident and universal truth.

That every effect must have a cause, is the maxim upon which the necessitarian takes his stand, and from which he delights to draw his favourite conclusion. It may be well, therefore, to examine the argument which has been so frequently erected upon the maxim in question. Although from various considerations, it has been very justly concluded, that there is somewhere a lurking fallacy in the argument, yet it has not been precisely shown where the fallacy lies. Suspicion has been thrown over it: nay, abundant reason has been shown why it should be rejected; but yet the fallacy of it should be dragged from the place of its concealment, and laid open in a clear light, so as to render it apparent to every eye. If it is a sophism, it certainly can be exposed, and it should be done.

In order to do this, it will be necessary to consider the nature and use of the maxim, that every effect must have a cause. I am aware, that no necessitarian of the present day, would choose to express this maxim as I have expressed it; for in such a form Mr. Hume has shown that it contains no information, and is indeed a most insignificant proposition. And, in truth, what does it amount to? Cause and effect are correlative terms; and when we speak of an effect, we mean something that is produced by a cause; and hence, the famous proposition, that every effect has a cause, amounts only to this, that every effect is an effect!

After Mr. Hume had caused the subject to be viewed in this light, the usual mode of expression was dropped; and it has now become the common practice to say, that there is no change in nature without a cause. But I do not see how this mends the matter *in the least:* it may disguise, but it does not alter the nature or real import of the maxim in question. For when it is said that every change has a cause, it is evident that a change is conceived of under the idea of an effect. It is supposed to be produced by a cause, and therefore it must be considered as an effect; and if the idea remains precisely the same, I do not see that giving it a new name, can possibly make any difference in the meaning of the proposition.

The maxim, that every effect must have a cause, is a self-evident and universal proposition. Its truth is involved in the very definition of the terms of which it is composed. In this respect it is like the axioms of geometry. When it is said, for example, that "the whole is equal to the sum of the parts," we at once perceive the truth of the axiom; because the "whole" is merely another name for "the sum of the parts." It is intuitively certain that they are equal, because they are but different expressions of the same thing. So, likewise, when it is affirmed, that every effect or every change in nature has a cause, we instantly perceive the truth of the proposition; inasmuch as an effect is that which is produced by a cause. The very idea of an effect implies its relation to a cause; and to say, that it has one, is only to say, that an effect is an effect. For if it were not produced by a cause, it would not be an effect.

The maxim under consideration is as unquestionably true as any axiom in Euclid. It does not depend for the evidence of its truth upon observation, or experience, or reasoning; it carries its own evidence along with it. No sooner are the terms in which it is expressed understood, than it rivets irresistible conviction on the mind. It is a fundamental law of belief; and it is impossible for the imagination of man to conceive, that an effect, or that which is produced by a cause, should be without a cause. And it were just as idle an employment of one's time, to undertake to prove such a proposition, as it would be to attempt to refute it.

Now, one of the fallacies of the argument of the necessitarian is, that it is an attempt to draw a conclusion from the axiomatical truth above referred to, as from the major of a syllogism. Every such attempt must necessarily be vain and fruitless. "Axioms," justly remarks Mr. Locke, "are not the foundations on which any of the sciences are built." And again, "It was not the influence of those maxims which are taken for principles in mathematics, that hath led the masters of that science into the wonderful discoveries they have made. Let a man of good parts know all the maxims generally made use of in mathematics never so perfectly, and contemplate their extent and consequences as much as he pleases, he will, by their assistance, I suppose, scarce ever come to know, that the square of the hypothenuse in a right-angled triangle, is equal to the squares of the two other sides. The knowledge, that the whole is equal to the parts, and, if you take equals from equals, the remainder will be equal, helped him not, I presume, to this demonstration. And a man may, I think, pore long enough on those axioms, without ever seeing one jot the more of mathematical truths."

The same doctrine is still more distinctly stated by Dugald Stewart. "If by the first principles of a science," says he, "be meant those fundamental propositions from which its remoter truths are derived, the axioms cannot, with any consistency, be called the first principles of mathematics. They have not, (it will be admitted,) the most distant analogy to what are called the first principles of natural philosophy:—to those general facts, for example, of the gravity and elasticity of the air, from which may be deduced, as consequences, the suspension of the mercury in the Torricellian tube, and its fall when carried up to an eminence. According to this meaning of the word, the first principles of mathematical science are, not the *axioms* but the *definitions*; which definitions hold, in mathematics, precisely the same place that is held in natural philosophy by such general facts as have now been referred to."

But the doctrine in question rests upon a firmer basis than that of human authority. Let any man examine the demonstrations in geometry, and attentively consider the principles from which the conclusions of that science are deduced, and he will find that they are *definitions*, and not *axioms*. He will find; that the properties of the triangle are derived from the definition of a triangle, and those of a circle from the definition of a circle. And then let him try his own skill upon the axioms of that science; let him arrange them and combine them in all possible ways; let him compare them together as long as he pleases, and determine for himself, whether they can be made to yield a single logical inference. If the question is thus brought to the test of an actual experience, I think it is not difficult to foresee, that the decision must be in favour of the doctrine of Stewart, and that it will be seen, that no such proposition as that whatever *is, is,* can even constitute the postulate, or first principle, in any sound argument; and that it is only from general facts, such as are ascertained by observation and experience, that we can derive logical consequences of any kind whatever, either in relation to matter or to mind.

If there is any truth in the foregoing remarks, or correctness in the position of Locke and Stewart, it is certainly one of the capital errors of Edwards, as well as of other necessitarians, that he has undertaken to deduce his doctrine from a metaphysical axiom, or identical proposition.

Supposing this to be the case, how has it happened, it may be asked, that the argument of the necessitarian has appeared so conclusive to himself, as well as unanswerable to others? The reason is plain. Having set out with a proposition, which is barren of all consequences, as the basis of his argument, it became necessary, in order to arrive at the destined conclusion, to assume, somewhere and somehow, in the course of his reasoning, the very point which he had undertaken to prove. Accordingly, this has been done; and the tacit assumption of the point in dispute seems not to have been suspected by him.

The justice of this remark may be shown, by a reference to the argument of the necessitarian. When this is reduced to the form of a syllogism, it stands thus: Every effect has a cause; a volition is an effect; and, therefore, a volition has a cause. In the middle term, which assumes that a volition is an effect, the point in dispute is taken for granted, the whole question is completely begged.

If we take the words in any sense, yet as they are correlative terms, the maxim that every effect must have a cause is self-evident; and hence, no conclusion can be drawn from it, unless the conclusion intended to be drawn is assumed in the middle term of the syllogism. It either begs the question, or it decides nothing to the purpose. It is true, that every change in nature must have a cause; that is to say, it is in some sense of the word an effect, and consequently must have a corresponding cause; but in what sense does every act of the mind come under the idea and definition of an effect? This is the question. Is it brought to pass by the prior action of motive? Is it necessitated? Upon this precise question, the maxim that every change must have a cause can throw no light; it only seems to refer to this point, by means of the very convenient ambiguity of the terms in which it is expressed. The necessitarian never fails to avail himself of this ambiguity. He seems both to himself and to the spectator to be carrying on a "great demonstration;" and this is one reason, perhaps, why the mind is diverted from the sophistical tricks, the metaphysical jugglery, by which both are deceived. Let us look a little more narrowly at this pretended demonstration.

The maxim in question is applied to volition; every change in nature, even the voluntary acts of the mind, must have a cause. Now according to Edwards' explanation of the term, this is a proposition which, I will venture to say, no man in his right mind ever ventured to deny. It is true, that President Edwards tells us of those, who "imagine that a volition has no cause, or *that it produces itself*;" and he has very well compared this to the absurdity of supposing, "that I gave myself my own being, or that I came into being without a cause," p. 277. But who ever held such a doctrine? Did any man, in his right mind, ever contend that "a volition could produce itself," can arise out of nothing, and bring itself into existence? If so, they were certainly beyond the reach of logic; they stood in need of the physician. I have never been so unfortunate as to meet with any advocate of free-agency, either in actual life or in history, who supposed that a volition arose out of nothing, without *any cause* of its existence, or that it produced itself. They have all maintained, with one consent, that the mind is the cause of volition. Is the mind nothing? If a man should say, as so many have said, that the mind produces its own volitions, is that equivalent to saying, that nothing produces

41

it; that it comes "into being accidentally, without any cause of its being?" Such is the broad caricature of their doctrine, which is repeatedly given by President Edwards.

It is freely admitted, and the advocates of free-agency have always admitted, that volition has a cause, as that word is frequently used by Edwards. He tells us, that by cause he sometimes means any antecedent, whether it exerts any positive influence or no. Now, in this sense, it is conceded by the advocates of free-agency, that motive itself is the cause of volition. This is the question: Is motive the efficient, or producing cause of volition? This is the question, I say; but Edwards frequently loses sight of it in a mist of ambiguities; and he lays around him in the dark, with such prodigious strength, that if his adversaries were not altogether imaginary beings, and therefore impassible to his ponderous blows, I have no doubt he would have slain more of them than ever Samson did of the Philistines.

The manner in which the necessitarian speaks of cause in his maxims, and reasonings, and pretended demonstrations, is of very great service to him. It includes, as we are told, every condition or cause of volition; (what a heterogeneous mass!) every thing without which volition could not come to pass. Yea, it is used in this sense, when it is said that motive is the cause of volition. What shall we do, then, with this broad, this most ambiguous proposition? Shall we deny it? If so, then we deny that volition has any cause of its existence, and fall into the great absurdity of supposing "volition to produce itself." Shall we assent to it, then? If so, we really admit that motive is the efficient cause of volition; and thus, by denying, we are made to reject our own doctrine, while, by affirming, we are made to receive that of our opponents. This way of proposing the doctrine of necessity very strongly reminds one of a certain trick in legislation, by which such things are forced into a bill, that in voting upon it, you must either reject what you most earnestly desire, or else sanction and support what you most earnestly detest. We should, therefore, neither affirm nor deny the whole proposition as it is set forth by the necessitarian; we should touch it with the dissecting knife, and cure it of its manifold infirmities.

The ambiguity of the term cause is, indeed, one of the most powerful weapons, both of attack and defence, in the whole armory of the necessitarian. Do you affirm the mind to be the cause of volition? Then, forthwith, as if the word could have only one meaning, it is alleged, that if the mind is the cause of volition, it can cause it only by a preceding volition; and so on *ad infinitum*. Hence, your doctrine must needs be absurd; because the word is understood, yea, and will be understood, in its most restrained and narrow sense. But do you deny motive to be the cause of volition? Then, how absurd are you again; you are no longer understood to use the word in the same sense; you now mean, not only that motive is not the producing cause of volition, but that there is absolutely nothing upon which it depends for its existence, and that "it produces itself." Does Edwards affirm that motive is the cause of volition; that motive causes volition to arise and come forth into existence; that it is not merely "the negative occasion" thereof, but the cause in the most proper sense of the word; that it is "the effectual power which produces volition?" What then? Dare you assert, in the face of such teaching, that motive is not the cause of volition? If so, then you are a most obstinate and perverse caviller; and you are silenced by the information that he *sometimes* uses the word cause to signify any antecedent, whether it has any positive influence or no. Yea, he gives this information, he declares, to "cut off occasion from any that might seek occasion to cavil and object against his doctrine," p. 51. These, and many other things of the same kind, are to be found in the writings of Day, and Edwards, and Collins, and Hobbes; and whosoever may be pleased to follow them, through all the doublings and windings of their logic, may do so at his leisure. It is sufficient for my present purpose to remark, that Edwards has included a number of different ideas in his definition of cause; and that he turns from the one to the other of these ideas, just as it suits the exigencies of his argument. It is in this way, as we have seen, that the famous maxim, that every change in nature must have a cause, has been made to serve his purpose.

He did not look at a volition and an effect, so as to mark their differences narrowly, and to proceed in his reasonings according to them; he set out with the great and universal truth, that every change in the universe must have a cause; from which lofty position the differences of things in this nether world were invisible. Having secured this position to his entire satisfaction, being firmly persuaded in his own mind, that "nonentity could not bring forth," he supposed he had gained a strong foothold; and from thence he proceeded to reason downward to what actually takes place in this lower world!

We are but "the humble servants and interpreters of nature," and we "can understand her operations only in so far as we have observed them." The necessitarian takes higher ground than this. He disdains the humble and patient task of observation. He plants his foot upon an eternal and immutable axiom; and, turning away from the study of what is, he magisterially pronounces what *must be.*

It is easy to see how he constructs his system. Every change in nature must have a cause, says he; this is very true; there is no truth in the world

43

more certain, according to the sense in which he frequently understands it. If he means to assert, that nothing, whether it be an entity, or an attribute, or a mode, can bring itself into existence, no one disputes his doctrine. It is most true, that there can be no choice without a mind that chooses, or an object in view of which it chooses; a mind, an object, and a desire, (if you please,) are the indispensable prerequisites, the invariable antecedents, to volition; but there is an immense chasm between this position and the doctrine, that the mind cannot put forth a volition, unless it is made to do so by the action of something else upon it. This immense chasm, the necessitarian can cross only by stepping over from one branch of his ambiguous proposition to another; he either does this, or he does not reach the point in controversy at all.

SECTION VII.

OF THE APPLICATION OF THE MAXIM THAT EVERY EFFECT MUST HAVE A CAUSE.

IN the last section I considered the application of the maxim, "that every effect must have a cause," to the question of necessity. This maxim figures so largely in every scheme of necessity, and it is relied upon with so much confidence, that I shall present some further views respecting its true nature and application. The necessitarian may see the truth of this maxim clearly, but he applies it vaguely.

He is always saying, "that if we give up this great principle of common sense, then there is no reasoning from effect to cause; and we cannot prove the existence of a God." Now I propose to show that we need not give up "this great principle of common sense;" that we may continue to reason from effect to cause, and so reach the conclusion that there is a God, by one of the most incontrovertible of all our mental processes; and yet we may, with perfect consistency, refuse to apply the maxim in question to human actions or volitions. In other words, that we may freely admit the principle in question, and yet reject the application which the necessitarian is accustomed to make of it.

In order to do this in a perspicuous and satisfactory manner, let us consider the occasion on which we first became acquainted with the truth of the principle, that every effect must have a cause. Let us consider the circumstances under which it is first suggested to the mind. Whence, then, do we derive the ideas of cause and effect, and of the necessary connection between them?

Locke, it is well known, supposed that we might derive the idea of causation by reflecting on the changes which take place in the external world. The fallacy of this supposition has been fully shown by Hume, and Brown, and Consin. In the refutation of Locke's notion, these celebrated philosophers were undoubtedly right; but the two first were wrong in the conclusion that we have no idea of power at all. Because the ideas of power and causation are not suggested by the changes of the material world, it does not follow that we have no such ideas in reality; that the only notion we have of causation is that of an invariable antecedence.

The only way in which the mind ever comes to be furnished with the ideas of cause and effect at all is this: we are conscious that we will a certain motion in the body, and we discover that the motion follows the volition. It is this act of the mind, this exertion of the will, that gives us the idea of a cause; and the change which it produces in the body, is that from which we derive

45

the idea of an effect. If we had never experienced a volition, we should never have formed the idea of causation. The idea of positive efficiency, or active power, would never have entered into our minds.

The two terms of the sequence, with which we are thus furnished by an actual experience, is an act of the mind, or a volition, on the one hand, which we call an efficient cause; and a modification or change in inert, passive matter, on the other, which we call an effect. It is easy to see how we rise from this single experience to the universal maxim in question. We are so made and constituted, by the Author of our nature, that we cannot help believing in the uniformity of nature's laws, or sequences. Hence, whenever we see either term of the above sequence, we are necessarily compelled, by a fundamental law of belief, to infer the existence of the other.

This fundamental law of belief, by which we repose the most implicit confidence in the uniformity of nature's sequences, has been recognized by many distinguished writers in modern times. It is well stated and illustrated by Dr. Chalmers. "The doctrine of innate ideas in the mind," says he, "is wholly different from the doctrine of innate tendencies in the mind—which tendencies may lie undeveloped till the excitement of some occasion have manifested or brought them forth. In a newly-formed mind, there is no idea of nature, or of a single object in nature; yet, no sooner is an object presented, or is an event observed to happen, than there is elicited the tendency of the mind to presume on the constancy of nature. At least as far back as our observation extends, the law of the mind is in full operation. Let an infant, for the first time in his life, strike on the table with a spoon; and, pleased with the noise, it will repeat that stroke with every appearance of a confident expectation that the noise will be repeated also. It counts on the invariableness wherewith the same consequent will follow the same antecedent. In the language of Dr. Thomas Brown, these two terms make up a sequence, and there seems to exist in the spirit of man not an underived, but an aboriginal faith in the uniformity of nature's sequences."—Nat. Theo. p. 121.

Now, the two terms which we find connected in the case before us, is an act of the mind, and a change or modification of the body. The volition is the antecedent, and the motion of body is the consequent. And these two, by virtue of the law of belief above stated, we shall always expect to find conjoined. Wherever we discover a change or modification, for example, in the corporeal system of any other person, similar to that which results from our own volitions, we shall necessarily infer the existence of a prior act by which it was produced.

Hence, when we witness a change *in the world of matter*, we are authorized to apply the maxim we have derived in the manner above explained. We have really no idea of an efficient cause, except that which we have derived from the phenomena of action. Hence, if we would not suffer ourselves to be imposed upon by words without meaning, when we see any change or effect in the material world, we should conclude that it proceeds from an action of spirit. When we see the same consequent, we should infer the existence of the same antecedent; and not suffer our minds to be confused and misled by the manifold ambiguities of language, as well as by the innumerable illusions of the fancy. Wherever we see a change in matter, we should infer an act by which it is produced; and thus, through all the changes and modifications of the material universe, we shall behold the sublime manifestations of an ever-present and all-pervading agency of spirit.

By a similar process, we are made acquainted with the existence of an intelligent and designing First Cause. We learn the connection between the adaptation of means to an end, and the operations of a designing mind, by reflecting on what passes within ourselves when we plan and execute a work of skill and contrivance. And, as we are so made as to rely with implicit confidence on the uniformity of nature's sequences; so, without further experience or induction, it is impossible for us to conceive of any contrivance whatever, without conceiving of it as proceeding from the hand of a contriver. Thus, we necessarily rise from the innumerable and wonderful contrivances in nature, to a belief in the existence of an intelligent and designing mind. In like manner may we establish the other attributes of God.

But to return to our maxim. We can only infer, from a change or modification in matter, the existence of an act by which it is produced. The former is the only idea we have of an effect; the latter is the only idea we have of an efficient cause. Hence, in reasoning from effect to cause, we can only reason from a change or modification in matter, or in that what is passive, to the act of some active power. This lays a sufficient foundation on which to rest the proof of the existence of God, as well as the existence of other minds.

But the case is very different when we turn from the contemplation of a *passive result* to consider an *efficient cause*—when we turn from the *motion of body* to consider the *activity of mind*. In such a case, the consequent ceases to be the same; and hence we have no right to infer that the antecedent is the same. We are conscious of an act; we perceive that it is followed by a change in the outward world; and henceforth, whenever we observe another change in the outward world, we are compelled to ascribe it, also, to a similar cause. This conviction results from the constitution of our minds—from a fundamental law of belief. But when we contemplate, not a change in the outward world, in that which is passive, but an act of the mind itself, the case is entirely different. We have some experience that certain changes in matter are the results of certain acts; and hence, whenever we observe similar phenomena, we are under a necessity of our nature to refer them to similar causes. We merely rely upon our veritable belief in the uniformity of nature's sequences, without a reliance upon which there can be no such thing as reasoning, when we ascend from the changes in the outward world to a belief in the agency of an efficient Cause. But we have no experience that an act of the mind is produced by a preceding act of the mind, or by the prior action of any thing else. President Edwards himself admits that our experience is silent on this subject. And hence, when we witness an act of the mind, or when we are conscious of a volition, our instinctive belief in the uniformity of nature's sequences does not require us to believe that it has an efficient cause; or, in other words, that it is produced by the prior action of something else, as the motion of body is produced by a prior act of mind. *A change in body* necessarily implies the prior action of something else by which it is produced; *an act of mind* only implies the existence of an agent that is capable of acting. Wherever an act exists, we must believe that there is a soul, or mind, or agent, that is capable of acting. We need not suppose that, like a change in body, it is brought to pass by a prior act. In other words, a change in that which is by nature passive, necessarily implies an act by which it is produced. But an act of the mind itself, which is not passive, does not likewise imply a preceding act by which it is produced. *It only implies the existence of an agent that is capable of acting, and the circumstances necessary to action as conditions, not as causes.*

Herein, then, lies the error of the necessitarian. He discovers from experience the connection between an act and a corresponding motion; and his instinctive belief in the uniformity of nature's sequences authorizes him to extend this connection to all sequences where the two terms are the same. That is to say, wherever he discovers a change in body, he is authorized to infer the existence of a prior act by which it was produced. But he does not confine himself to this sequence alone. He does not rest satisfied with the universal principle, that every change in body, or in that which is passive, must proceed from the prior action of something else. He makes a most unwarrantable extension of this principle. He supposes not only that every change in body, but also that every act of mind, must proceed from the prior action of something else. Thus he confounds passion and action. He takes it for granted that a volition is an *effect*—an effect in such a sense that it cannot proceed from the mind, unless it be produced by the prior act thereof. He asserts that "the mind cannot be the cause of such an effect," of a volition, "except by the preceding action of the mind." Thus, in rising from a single experience to a universal maxim, by virtue of our belief in the uniformity of nature's laws, he does not confine himself to the observed sequences; he does not keep his attention steadily fixed on a change in body as the consequent, and on an act as the invariable antecedent. On the contrary, from the exceedingly abstruse and subtle nature of the subject, as well as from the ambiguity of language, he treats a volition as a consequent, which implies the same kind of antecedent as does a change in body. Thus, by this unwarrantable extension or application of his principle, he confounds the *motion of body* with the *action of spirit*; than which there could hardly be a more unphilosophical confusion of ideas.

From the foregoing remarks, it will be perceived, as I have already said, that the question is not, *whether every effect must have a cause.* This is conceded. We do not give up "this great principle of common sense." We insist upon it as firmly as do our adversaries; and hence, we have as strong a foundation whereon to rest our belief in the being of a God. But the question is, *whether every cause is an effect?* Or, in other words, whether an act of mind can exist without being produced by the prior action of something else; just as the motion of body is produced by the prior action of mind? We say that it can exist without any such producing cause.

If it were otherwise, if every cause were an effect in the sense in which a volition is assumed to be an effect by the necessitarian, what would be the consequence? It is evident, that each and every cause in the universe must itself have a cause—must itself result from the preceding action of something else; and thus we should be involved in the great absurdity of an infinite series of causes, as well as in the iron scheme of an all-pervading necessity. But, happily, there is nothing in our experience, nor in any law of our nature, nor in both together, which requires us to believe that a volition is an effect in any such sense of the word. Call it an effect, if you please; but then it must be conceded that it is not, like the motion of body, such a consequent as necessarily requires the prior action of something else for its production.

Every *effect* must have a cause, it is true; but it is purely a gratuitous assumption—a mere *petitio principii*, to take it for granted that a volition is an effect in the sense in which the word should always be understood in this celebrated maxim. This maxim is undoubtedly true, as we have seen, when applied to the changes of that which cannot act: it is in reference to such effects, or consequents, that the conviction of its truth is first suggested; and we cannot doubt of the propriety of its application to all such effects, unless we can doubt of the uniformity of nature's sequences. But when we go over from the region of inert, passive matter, into that which is full of spiritual vigour and unceasing activity, and apply this maxim here in all its rigour, we do make a most unwarrantable extension of it. We pervert it from its true meaning and import; we identify volition with local motion; we involve ourselves in the greatest of all absurdities, as well as in the most ruinous of all doctrines.

As we have already said, then, we do not give up the great principle of common sense, that every effect must have a cause. We recognize this principle when we reason from effect to cause—when we ascend from the creation up to the Creator. We deny that volition is an effect; and what then? If volition be not an effect, are there no effects in the universe? Are we sunk in utter darkness? Have we no platform left whereon to stand, and to behold the glory of God, our Creator and Preserver? Surely we have. Every change throughout inanimate nature bespeaks the agency of Him, who "sits concealed behind his own creation," but is everywhere manifested by his omnipresent energy. The human body is an effect, teeming with evidences of the most wonderful skill of its Great Cause and Contriver. The soul itself is an effect,— the soul, with all its complicated and wonder-working powers, is an effect; and clearly proclaims the wisdom, and the goodness, and the holiness of its Maker. The heavens above us, with all its shining hosts and admirable mechanism, proclaims the glory of God; and the whole universe of created intelligences shout for joy, as they respond in their eternal anthems to the "music of the spheres." And is not this enough? Is the whole psaltery of heaven and earth marred, and all its sweet harmony turned into harsh discord, if we only dare to assert that an act is not an effect? No, no: this too proclaims the glory of God; for, however great may be the mystery, it only shows that the Almighty has called into existence innumerable creatures, bearing the impress of his own glorious image, and that, in consequence thereof, they are capable of acting without being compelled to act.

It is the position of Edwards, and not ours, that would disprove the existence of a God. We believe in action which is uncaused by any prior action; and hence, we can reason from effects up to Cause, and there find a resting-place. We do not look beyond that which is uncaused. We believe there is action somewhere, uncaused by preceding action; and if we did not believe this, we should be constrained to adopt the doctrine of Edwards, that action itself must be caused "by the action of something else," p. 203; which necessarily lands us in an infinite series of causes; the very ground occupied by Atheists in all ages of the world. It is well, therefore, to hold on to "this great principle of common sense, that every effect must have a cause," in order that we may rise from the world and its innumerable wonders to the contemplation of the infinite wisdom and goodness of God: it is also well that we should hold it with a distinction, and not apply it to action, in order that we may not be forced beyond the Great First Cause—the central light of the Universe, into the "outer darkness" of the old atheistic scheme of an infinite series of causes. If we give up this principle, we cannot prove the existence of a God, it is most true; but yet, if we apply this principle as Edwards applies it, we are irresistibly launched upon an infinite series of causes, and compelled to shoot entirely beyond the belief of a God. We quarrel not, therefore, with his great principle; but we utterly reject his application of it, as leading directly to Atheism.

SECTION VIII.

OF THE RELATION BETWEEN THE FEELINGS AND THE WILL.

It is well known that Edwards confounds the sensitive part of our nature with the will, the susceptibility by which the mind feels with the power by which it acts. He expressly declares, that "the affections and the will are not two faculties of the soul;" and it is upon this confusion of things that much of his argument depends for its coherency.

But although he thus expressly confounds them; yet he frequently speaks of them, in the course of his argument, as if they were two different faculties of the soul. Thus, he frequently asserts that the will is determined by "the strongest appetite," by "the strongest disposition," by "the strongest inclination." Now, in these expressions, he evidently means to distinguish appetite, inclination, and disposition, from the will; and if he does not, then he asserts, that the will is determined by itself, a doctrine which he utterly repudiates.

The soundness of much of his argument depends, as I have said, upon the confusion or the identification of these two properties of the mind; the soundness of much of it also depends upon the fact that they are not identical, but distinct. From a great number of similar passages, we may select the following, as an illustration of the justness of this remark: "Moral necessity," says he, "may be as *absolute*, as natural necessity. That is, the effect may be as powerfully connected with its moral cause, as a natural necessary effect is with its natural cause. Whether the will in every case is necessarily determined by the strongest motive, or whether the will ever makes any resistance to such a motive, or can ever oppose the strongest present inclination, or not; if that matter should be controverted, yet I suppose none will deny, but that, in some cases, a previous bias, or inclination, or the motive presented, may be SO POWERFUL, THAT THE ACT OF THE WILL MAY BE CERTAINLY AND INDISSOLUBLY CONNECTED THEREWITH. When motives or previous bias are very strong, all will allow that there is some *difficulty* in going against them. And if they were yet stronger, the difficulty would be still greater. And, therefore, if more be still added to their strength, to a certain degree, it would make the difficulty so great, that it would be wholly *impossible* to surmount it; for, this plain reason, because whatever power men may be supposed to have to surmount difficulties, yet that power is not infinite; and so goes not beyond certain limits. If a man can surmount ten degrees of difficulty of this kind with twenty degrees of strength, because the degrees of strength are beyond the degrees of difficulty; yet if the difficulty be increased to thirty, or an hundred, or a thousand degrees, and his strength not also increased, his strength will be wholly insufficient to surmount the difficulty. As, therefore, it must be allowed, that there may be such a thing as a *sure* and *perfect* connexion between moral causes and effects; so this only is what I call by the name of *moral necessity.*"

Now he here speaks of inclination and previous bias, as elsewhere of appetite and disposition, as distinct from volition. In this he is right; even the necessitarian will not, at the present day, deny that our desires, affections, &c., are different from volition. "Between motive and volition," says President Day, "there must intervene an apprehension of the object, and *consequent feeling excited in the mind.*" Thus, according to President Day, feeling is not volition; it intervenes between the external object and volition. But although Edwards is right in this; there is one thing in which he is wrong. He is wrong in supposing that our feelings possess a real strength, by which they act upon and control the will.

It is obvious that the coherency and force of the above passage depends on the idea, that there is a real power in the strongest inclination or desire of the mind, which renders it difficult to be surmounted or overcome. For if we suppose, that our inclinations or desires are merely the occasions on which we act, and that they themselves exert no influence or efficiency in the production of our volitions, it would be absurd to speak of the difficulty of overcoming them, as well as to speak of this difficulty as increasing with the increasing strength of the inclination, or desire. Take away this idea, show that there is no real strength in motives, or desires and inclinations, and the above extract will lose all its force; it will fall to pieces of itself.

Indeed, the idea or supposition in question, is one of the strongholds of the necessitarian. External objects are regarded as the efficient causes of desire; desire as the efficient cause of volition; and in this way, the whole question seems to be settled. The same result would follow, if we should suppose that desire is awakened not exclusively by external objects, but partly by that which is external, and partly by that which is internal. On this supposition, as well as on the former, the will would seem to be under the dominion of the strongest desire or inclination of the soul.

The assumption, that there is a real efficiency exerted by the desires and inclinations of the soul, has been, so far as I know, universally conceded to the necessitarian. He seems to have been left in the undisputed possession of this stronghold; and yet, upon mature reflection, I think we may find some reason to call it in question. If I am not greatly mistaken, we may see that the necessitarian has some reason to abate the loftiness of his tone, when he asserts, that "we *know* that the feelings do exert an influence in the production of volition." This may appear very evident to his mind; nay, at first view, it may appear very evident to all minds; and yet, after all, it may be only an "idol of the tribe."

It is a commonly received opinion, among philosophers, that the passions, desires, &c., do really exert an influence to produce volition. This was evidently the idea of Burlamaqui. He draws a distinction between voluntary actions and free actions; and as an instance of a voluntary action which is not free, he cites the case of a man who, as he supposes, is constrained to act from fear. He supposes that such an action, though voluntary, is not free, because it is brought about by the irresistible influence of the passion of fear.

It is believed, also, by the disciples of Butler, that there is a real strength possessed by what are called the "active powers" of the mind. "This distinction," says Dr. Chalmers, "made by the sagacious Butler between the power of a principle and its authority, enables us in the midst of all the actual anomalies and disorders of our state, to form a precise estimate of the place which conscience naturally and rightly holds in man's constitution. The desire of acting virtuously, which is a desire consequent on our sense of right and wrong, may not be of *equal strength* with the desire of some criminal indulgence, and so, practically, the evil may predominate over the good. And thus it is that the system of the inner man, from *the weakness* of that which claims to be the ascendant principle of our nature, may be thrown into a state of turbulence and disorder."—Nat. The. p. 313.

Such was the idea of Butler himself. He frequently speaks of the supremacy of conscience, in terms such as the following: "That principle by which we survey, and either approve or disapprove, our heart, temper, and actions, is not only to be considered as what in its turn is to have some influence, which may be said of every passion, of the basest appetite; but likewise as being superior; as from its very nature manifestly claiming superiority over all others; insomuch that you cannot form a notion of this faculty conscience, without taking in judgement, direction, and superintendency. This is a constituent part of the idea, that is of the faculty itself; and to preside and govern, from the very economy and constitution of man, belongs to it. Had it *might*, as it has right; had it *power*, as it has manifest authority; it would absolutely govern the world."

This language, it should be observed, is not used in a metaphorical sense; it occurs in the statement of a philosophical theory of human nature. Similar language is frequently to be found in the writings of the most enlightened advocates of free-agency. Thus, says Jouffroy, even while he is contending against the doctrine of necessity: "There are two kinds of *moving powers* acting upon us; first, the impulses of instinct, or passion; and, secondly, the conceptions of reason...... That these two kinds of moving powers can and do, act efficiently upon our volitions, there can be no doubt," p. 102. If it were necessary, it might be shown, by hundreds of extracts from their writings, that the great advocates of free-agency have held, that the emotions, desires, and passions, do really act on the will, and tend to produce volitions.

But why dwell upon particular instances? If any advocate of free-agency had really believed, that the passions, desires, affections, &c., exert no influence over the will, is it not certain that he would have availed himself of this principle? If the principle that no desire, or affection, or passion, is possessed of any power or causal influence, had been adopted by the advocates of free-agency, its bearing in favour of their cause would have been too obvious and too important to have been overlooked. The necessitarian might have supposed, if he had pleased, that our desires and affections are produced by the action of external objects; and yet, on the supposition that these exerted no positive or causal influence, the doctrine of liberty might have been most successfully maintained. For, after all, the desires and affections thus produced in the mind, would not, on the supposition in question, be the causes of our volitions. They would merely be the occasions on which we act. There would be no necessary connexion between what are called motives and their corresponding actions. Our desires or emotions might be under the influence and dominion of external causes, or of causes that are partly external and partly internal; but yet our volitions would be perfectly free from all preceding influences whatever. Our volitions might depend on certain conditions, it is true, such as the possession of certain desires or affections; but they would not result from the influence or action of them. They would be absolutely free and uncontrolled. The reason why this principle has not been employed by the advocates of free-agency is, I humbly conceive, because it has not been entertained by them.

In short, if the advocates of free-agency had shaken off the common illusion that there is a real efficiency, or causal influence, exerted by the desires of the soul, they would have made it known in the most explicit and unequivocal terms. Instead of resorting to the expedients they have adopted, in order to surmount the difficulties by which they have been surrounded, they would, every where and on all occasions, have reminded their adversaries that those difficulties arise merely from ascribing a literal signification to language, which is only true in a metaphorical sense; and we should have had pages, not to say volumes, concerning this use of language, where we have not had a syllable.

If the illusion in question has been as general as I have supposed, it is not difficult to account for its prevalence. The fact that a desire, or affection is the indispensable condition, the invariable antecedent, of an act of the will, is of itself sufficient to account for the prevalence of such a notion. Nothing is more common than for men to mistake an invariable antecedent for an efficient cause. This source of error, it is well known, has given rise to some of the most obstinate delusions that have ever infested and enslaved the human mind.

And besides, when such an error or illusion prevails, its hold upon the mind is confirmed and rendered almost invincible by the circumstance, that it is interwoven into the structure of all our language. In this case in particular, we never cease to speak of "the active principles," of "the ruling passion," of "ungovernable desire," of "the dominion of lust," of being "enslaved to a vicious propensity;"—in a thousand ways, the idea that there is a real efficiency in the desires and affections of the soul, is wrought into the structure of our language; and hence, there is no wonder that it has gained such an ascendency over our thoughts. It has met us at every turn; it has presented itself to us in a thousand shapes; it has become so familiar, that we have not even stopped to inquire into its true nature. Its dominion has become complete and secure, just because its truth has never been doubted.

The illusion in question, if it be one, has derived an accession of strength from another source. It is a fact, that whenever we feel intensely, we do, as a general thing, act with a proportioned degree of energy; and *vice versa*. Hence, we naturally derive the impression, that the determinations of the will are produced by the strength of our feelings. If the passion or desire is languid, (since we must use a metaphor,) the action is in general feeble; and if it is intense, the act is *usually* powerful and energetic. Hence, we are prone to conclude, that the mind is moved to act by the influence of passion or desire; and that the energy of the action corresponds with the strength of the motive, or moving principle.

Though the principle in question has been so commonly received, I think we should be led to question it in consequence of the conclusions which have been deduced from it. If our desires, affections, &c., operate to influence the will, how can it be free in putting forth volitions? How does Mr. Locke meet this difficulty? Does he tell us, that it arises solely from our mistaking a metaphorical for a literal mode of expression? Far from it.

He does not place liberty on the broad ground, that the desires by which volitions are supposed to be determined, are in reality nothing more than the conditions or occasions on which the mind acts; and that they themselves can exert no positive influence or efficiency. The liberty of the soul consists, according to him, not in the circumstance that its desires do not *operate*, but in its power to arrest the operation of its desires. He admits that they operate, that they tend to produce volition; but the mind is nevertheless free, because it can suspend the operation of desire, and prevent the tendency thereof from passing into effect. "There being," says he, "in us a great many uneasinesses always soliciting and ready to determine the will, it is natural, as I have said, that the greatest or most pressing should determine the will to the next action; and so it does for the most part, but not always. For the mind having in most cases, as is evident in experience, a power to suspend the execution and satisfaction of its desires, and so all, one after another, examine them on all sides, and weigh them with others. In this lies the liberty man has."

Thus we are supposed to be free, because we have a power to resist, in some cases at least, the influence of desire. But this is not always the case. Our desires may be so strong as entirely to overcome us—and what then? Why we cease to be free agents; and it is only when the storm of passion subsides, that we are restored to the rank of accountable beings. "Sometimes a boisterous passion hurries away our thoughts," says Locke, "as a hurricane does our bodies, without leaving us the liberty of thinking on other things, which we would rather choose. But as soon as the mind regains the power to stop or continue, begin or forbear, any of these motives of the body without, or thoughts within, according as it thinks fit to prefer either to the other, we then consider the man as a free-agent again." This language is employed by Mr. Locke, while attempting to define the idea of liberty or free-agency; and he evidently supposed, as appears from the above passage, as well as from some others, that we frequently cease to be free-agents, in consequence of the irresistible power of our desires or passions.

Dr. Reid set out from the same position, and he arrived at the same conclusion. He frequently speaks of the appetites and passions as so many forces, whose action is "directly upon the will." "They draw a man towards a certain object, without any further view, by a sort of violence."—Essays, p. 18. "When a man is acted upon by motives of this kind, he finds it easy to yield to the strongest. They are like two forces pushing him in contrary directions. To yield to the strongest, he need only be passive," p. 237. "In actions that proceed from appetite and passion, we are passive in part and only in part active. They are therefore in part imputed to the passion; and if it is supposed to be irresistible, we do not impute them to the man at all. Even an American savage judges in this way; when in a fit of drunkenness he kills his friend; as soon as he comes to himself, he is very sorry for what he has done, but pleads that drink, and not he, was the cause," p. 14, 15. Such is the dreadful consequence, which Dr. Reid boldly deduces from the principle, that the appetites and passions do really act upon the will. Though he was an advocate of free-agency; yet, holding this principle, he could speak of *actions that are partly passive;* and that in so far as they are passive, he maintained they should not be imputed to the man whose actions they are, but to the passions by which they are produced, This may appear to be strange doctrine for an advocate of free-agency and accountability; but it seems to be the natural and inevitable consequence of the commonly received notion with respect to the relation which subsists between the passions and the will.

The principle that our appetites, desires, &c., do exert a real influence in the production of volition, was common to Edwards, Locke, and Reid: indeed, so far as I know, it has been universally received. In the opinion of Edwards, this influence becomes "so powerful" at times as to establish a moral necessity beyond all question; and in that of Locke and Reid, it is sometimes so great as to destroy free-agency and accountability. Is not this inference well drawn? It seems to me that it is; and this constitutes one reason, why I deny the principle from which it is deduced.

Is it true, then, that any power or efficacy belongs to the sensitive or emotive part of our nature? Reflection must show us, I think, that it is absurd to suppose that any desire, affection, or disposition of the mind, can really and truly exert any positive or productive influence. When we speak of the appetites, desires, affections, &c., as the "active principles" of our nature, we must needs understand this as a purely metaphorical mode of expression.

Edwards himself has shown the impropriety of regarding similar modes of speech as a literal expression of the truth. "To talk of liberty," says he, "or the contrary, as belonging to the *very will itself,* is not to speak good sense; if we judge of sense, and nonsense, by the original and proper signification of words. For the will *itself* is not an agent that *has a will:* the power of choosing, itself, has not a power of choosing. That which has the power of volition is the man, or the soul, and not the power of volition itself. To be free is the property of an agent, who is possessed of powers and faculties, as much as to be cunning, valiant, bountiful, or zealous. But *these qualities are the properties of persons*, and not the *properties of properties.*" This remark, no doubt, is perfectly just, as well as highly important. And it may be applied with equal force and propriety, to the practice of speaking of the strength of motives, or inclinations, or desires; for power is a "property of the person, or the soul; and not the property of a property."

It appeared exceedingly absurd to the author of the "Inquiry," to speak of "the free acts of the will," as being *determined by the will itself;* because the *will* is not an agent, and "actions are to be ascribed to agents, and not properly to the powers and properties of agents." But he seemed to perceive no absurdity, in speaking of "the free acts of the will," as being caused by the strongest motives, by the dispositions and appetites of the soul. Now, are the strongest motives, as they are called, are the strongest dispositions and desires of the soul, agents, or are they merely the properties of agents? Let the necessitarian answer this question, and then determine whether his logic is consistent with itself.

Mr. Locke, also, has well said, that it is absurd to inquire whether "the will be free or no; inasmuch as *liberty*, which is but a *power*, belongs only to agents, and cannot be an attribute or modification of will, which is also but a power." Though Mr. Locke applied this remark to the usual form of speech, by which freedom is ascribed to the will, he failed to do so in regard to the language by which power, which is a property of the mind itself, is ascribed to our desires, or passions, or affections, which are likewise properties of the mind. And hence have arisen many of his difficulties in regard to the freedom of human actions. Supposing that our desires exerted some positive influence or efficiency in the production of volitions, his views on the subject of free-agency become vague, inconsistent, fluctuating and unsatisfactory.

The hypothesis that the desires impel the will to act, is inconsistent with observed facts. If this hypothesis were true, the phenomena of volition would be very different from what they are. A man may desire that it should rain, for example; he may have the most intense feeling on this subject imaginable, and there may be no counteracting desire or feeling whatever; now if desire ever impelled a man to volition, it would induce him, in such a case, to will that it should rain. But no man, in his senses, ever puts forth a volition to make it rain—and why? Just because he is a rational creature, and knows that his volition cannot produce any such effect. In the same manner, a man might wish to fly, or to do a thousand other things which are beyond his power; and yet not make the least effort to do so, not because he has no power to put forth such efforts, but because he does not choose to make a fool of himself: This shows that desire, feeling, &c., is merely one of the conditions necessary to volition, and not its producing cause.

Again. It has been frequently observed, since the time of Butler, that our passive impressions often become weaker and weaker, while our active habits become stronger and stronger. Thus, the feeling of pity, by being frequently excited, may become less and less vivid, while the active habit of benevolence, by which it is supposed to be induced, becomes more and more energetic. That is to say, while the power, as it is called, or the causal influence, is gradually diminishing, the effect, which is supposed to flow from it, is becoming more and more conspicuous. And again, the feeling of pity is sometimes exceedingly strong; that is to say, exceedingly vivid and painful, while there is no act attending it. The passive impression or susceptibility is entirely dissociated, in many cases, from the acts of the will. The feeling often exists in all its *power*, and yet there is no act, and no disposition to act, on the part of the individual who is the subject of it. The cause operates, and yet the effect does not follow!

All that we can say is, that when we see the mind deeply agitated, and, as it were, carried away by a storm of passion, we also observe that it frequently acts with great vehemency. But we do not observe, and we do not know, that this increased *power of action*, is the result of an increased *power of feeling*. All that we know is, that as a matter of fact, when our feelings are languid, we are apt to act but feebly; and that when they are intense, we are accustomed to act with energy. Or, in other words, that we do not *ordinarily* act with so much energy in order to gratify a slight feeling or emotion, as we do to gratify one of greater intensity and painfulness. But it is wrong to conclude from hence, that it is the increased intensity of feeling, which produces the increased energy of the action. No matter how intense the feeling, it is wrong to conclude, that it literally causes us to act, that it ever lays the will under constraint, and thereby destroys, even for a moment, our free-agency. Such an assumption is a mere hypothesis, unsupported by observation, inconsistent with the dictates of reason, and irreconcilable with observed facts.

I repeat it, such an assumption is inconsistent with observed facts; for who that has any energy of will, has not, on many a trying occasion, stood firm amid the fiercest storm of passion; and, though the elements of discord raged within, remained *himself* unmoved; giving not the least sign or manifestation of what was passing in his bosom? Who has not felt, on such an occasion, that although the passions may storm, yet the will alone is power?

It is not uncommon to see this truth indirectly recognized by those who *absolutely know* that some power is exerted by our passions and desires, and that the will is always determined by the strongest. Thus, says President Day, "our acts of choice, are *not* always controlled by those emotions which *appear to be most vivid*. We often find a determined and settled purpose, apparently calm, but unyielding, which carries a man steadily forward, amid all the solicitations of appetite and passion The inflexible determination of Howard, *gave law to his emotions*, and guided his benevolent movements," p. 65. Here, although President Day holds that the will is determined by the strongest desire, passion, or emotion, he unconsciously admits that the will, "the inflexible determination," is independent of them all.

Let it be supposed, that no one means so absurd a thing as to say, that the affections themselves act upon the will, but that the mind in the exercise of its affections acts upon it, and thereby exerts a power over its determinations; let us suppose, that this is the manner in which a real force is supposed to bear upon the will; and what will be the consequence? Why, if the will is not distinguished from the affections, we shall have the will acting upon itself; a doctrine to which the necessitarian will not listen for a moment. And if they are distinguished from the will, we shall have two powers of action, two forces in the mind, each contending for the mastery. But what do we mean by a will, if it is not the faculty by which the mind acts, by which it exerts a *real force?* And if this be the idea and definition of a will, we cannot distinguish the will from the affections, and say that the latter exerts a real force, without making two wills. This seems to be the inevitable consequence of the commonly received notion, that the mind, in the exercise of its affections, does really act upon the will with an impelling force. Indeed, there seems to have been no little perplexity and confusion of conception on this subject, arising from the extreme subtlety of our mental processes, as well as from the ambiguities of language.

The truth is, that in feeling the mind is passive; and it is absurd to make a passive impression, the active cause of any thing. The sensibility does not *act*, it merely *suffers*. The appetites and passions, which have always been called the "active powers," the "moving principles," and so forth, should be called the passive susceptibilities. Unless this truth be clearly and fully recognized, and the commonly received notion respecting the relation which the appetites and passions sustain to the will, to the *active power*, be discarded, it seems to me, that the great doctrine of the liberty of the will, must continue to be involved in the sadest perplexity, the most distressing darkness.

SECTION IX.

OF THE LIBERTY OF INDIFFERENCE.

IF, as I have endeavoured to show, the appetites and passions exert no positive influence in the production of volition, if they do not sustain the relation of cause to the acts of the will; then is the doctrine of the liberty of indifference placed in a clear and strong light having admitted that the sensitive part of our nature always tends to produce volition, and in some cases irresistibly produces it, the advocates of free agency have not been able to maintain the doctrine of a perfect liberty in regard to all human actions. They have been compelled to retire from the broad and open field of the controverted territory, and to take their stand in a dark corner, in order to contend for that perfect liberty, without which there cannot be a perfect and unclouded accountability. Hence, it has been no uncommon thing, even for those who have been the most disposed to sympathize with them, to feel a dissatisfaction in reading what they have written on the subject of a liberty of indifference. This they have placed in a perfect freedom to choose between a few insignificant things, in regard to which we have no feeling; while, in regard to the great objects which relate to our eternal destiny, we have been supposed to enjoy no such freedom.

The true liberty of indifference does not consist, as I have endeavoured to show, in a power to resist the influence of the appetites and passions struggling to produce volition; because there is no such influence in existence. This notion is encumbered with insuperable difficulties; it supposes two powers struggling for the mastery—the desires on the one hand, and the will on the other; and that when the desires are so strong as to prevail, and bear us away in spite of ourselves, we cease to be free agents. It supposes that at no time we have a perfect liberty, unless we are perfectly destitute of feeling; and that at some of the most trying, and critical, and awful moments of our existence, we have no liberty at all; the whole man being passive to the power and dominion of the passions. What a wound is thus given to the cause of free-agency and accountability! What scope is thus allowed for the sophistry of the passions! Every man who can persuade himself that his appetites, his desires, or his passions, have been too strong for him, may blind his mind to a sense of his guilt, and lull his conscience into a fatal repose.

The necessitarian, like a skilful general, is not slow to attack this weak point in the philosophy of free-agency. If our emotions operate to produce volition, says he, then the strongest must prevail; to say otherwise, is to say that it is not the strongest. This is the ground uniformly occupied by President Day. And it is urged by President Edwards, that if a great degree of such

62

influence destroys free agency, as it is supposed to do, then every smaller degree of it must impair free agency; and hence, according to the principles and scheme of its advocates, it cannot be perfect. Is not this inference well drawn? Indeed, it seems to me, that while the notion that our desires possess a real power and efficacy, which are exerted over the will, maintains its hold upon the mind, the great doctrine of liberty can never be seen in the brightness of its full-orbed glory; and that it must, at times, suffer a total eclipse.

The liberty which we really possess, then, does not consist in an indifference of the desires and affections, but in that of the will itself. We are perfectly free, says the libertarian, in regard to all those things about which our feelings are in a state of indifference; such as touching one of two spots, or choosing one of two objects that are perfectly alike. To this the necessitarian replies, what does it signify that a man has a perfect liberty in regard to the choice of "one of two peppercorns?" Are not such things perfectly insignificant, and unworthy "the grave attention of the philosopher," while treating of the great questions of moral good and evil?

There is some truth in this reply, and some injustice. It truly signifies nothing, that we are at perfect liberty to choose between two pepper-corns, if we are not so to choose between good and evil, life and death. But in making this attack upon the position of his opponent, when viewed as designed to serve the cause of free-agency, the necessitarian overlooks its bearing upon his own scheme. He contends, that the mind cannot act unless it is made to act by some extraneous influence: this is a universal proposition, extending to all our mental acts; and hence, if it can be shown that, in a single instance, the mind can and does put forth a volition, without being made to do so, his doctrine is subverted from its foundations. If this can be shown, by a reference to the case of "two pepper-corns," it may be made to serve an important purpose in philosophy, how much soever it may be despised by the philosopher.

If we keep the distinction between the will and the sensibility in mind, it will throw much light on what has been written in regard to the subject of indifference. If you offer a guinea and a penny to a man's choice, asks President Day, which will he choose? Will the one exert as great an influence over him as the other? President Day may assert, if he pleases, that the guinea will exert the greater influence over his feelings; but this does not destroy the equilibrium of the will. The feelings and the will are different. By the one we feel, by the other we act; by the one we *suffer*, by the other we *do*. Why, then, will the man be certain to choose the guinea, all other things being equal? Not because its influence acts upon the will, either directly or indirectly through the passions, and compels him to choose it, but because he has a purpose to accomplish; and, as a rational being, he sees that the guinea will answer his purpose better than the penny. He is not made to act, therefore, by a blind impulse; he acts freely in the light of reason. The philosophy of the necessitarian overlooks the slight circumstance, that the will of man is not a ball to be set a-going by external impulse; but that man is a rational being, made in the image of his Maker, and can act as a designing cause. Hence, when we affirm that the will of man acts without being made to do so by the action of any thing upon *the will itself*, he imagines that we dethrone the Almighty, and "place chance upon the throne of the moral universe." Day on the Will, p. 195. But I would remind him, once for all, that the act of a free designing cause, no less than that of a necessitated act, proceeding from an efficient cause, (if such a thing can be conceived,) is utterly inconsistent with the idea of accident. Choice in its very nature is opposed to chance.

The doctrine of the indifference of the will has been subjected to another mode of attack. This doctrine implies that we have a power to choose one thing or another; or, as it is sometimes called, a power of choice to the contrary. For, if the will is not controlled by any extraneous influence, it is evident that we may choose a thing, or let it alone—that we may put forth a volition, or refuse to put it forth. This power, which results from the idea of indifference as just explained, is regarded as in the highest degree absurd; and a torrent of impetuous questions is poured forth to sweep it away. "When Satan, as a roaring lion," asks President Day, "goeth about, seeking whom he may devour, is he equally inclined to promote the salvation of mankind?" &c. &c. &c. Now, I freely admit, that when Satan is inclined to do evil, and is actually doing it, he is not inclined to the contrary. I freely admit that a thing is not different from itself; and the learned author is welcome to all such triumphant positions.

In the same easy way, President Edwards, as he imagines, demolishes the doctrine of indifference. He supposes that, according to this doctrine, the will does not choose when it does choose; and, having supposed this, he proceeds to demolish it, as if he were contending with a thousand adversaries; and yet, I will venture to affirm, that no man in his senses ever maintained such a position. The most contemptible advocate of free-agency that ever lived, has maintained nothing so absurd as that the mind ever chooses without choosing. This is the light in which the doctrine of indifference is frequently represented by Edwards, but it is a gross misrepresentation.

"The question is," says Edwards, "whether ever the soul of man puts forth an act of will, while it yet remains in a state of liberty, viz: as implying a state of indifference; or whether the soul ever exerts an act of preference, while at the very time *the will* is in a perfect equilibrium, not inclining one way more than another," p. 72. If this be the point in dispute, he may well add, that "the very putting of the question is sufficient to show the absurdity of the affirmative answer;" and he might have added, the utter futility of the negative reply. "How ridiculous," he continues, "for any body to insist that the soul chooses one thing before another, when, at the very same instant, it is perfectly indifferent with respect to each! This is the same thing as to say, we shall prefer one thing to another, at the very same time that it has no preference. Choice and preference can no more be in a state of indifference than motion can be in a state of rest," &c. p. 72. And he repeats it over and over again, that this is to put "the soul in a state of choice, and in a state of equilibrium at the same time;" "choosing one way, while it remains in a state of perfect indifference, and has no choice of one way more than the other;" p. 74. "To suppose the will to act at all in a state of indifference, is to assert that the mind chooses without choosing," p. 64; and so in various other places.

Now, if the doctrine of the indifference of the will, as commonly understood, amounts to this, that the will does not choose when it chooses, then Edwards was certainly right in opposing it; but how could he have expected to correct such incorrigible blockheads as the authors of such a doctrine must have been, by the force of logic?

Edwards has not always, though frequently, mis-stated the doctrine of his adversaries. The liberty of indifference, says he, in one place, consists in this, "that the will, in choosing, is subject to *no prevailing* influence," p. 64. Now this is a fair statement of the doctrine in question. Why did not Edwards, then, combat this idea? Why transform it into the monstrous absurdity, that "the will chooses without choosing," or exerts an act of choice at the same time that it exerts no act of choice; and then proceed to demolish it? Was it because he did not wish to march up, fairly and squarely, in the face of the enemy, and contend with them in their strongholds and fastnesses? By no means. There never was a more honest reasoner than Edwards. But his psychology is false; and hence, he has not only misrepresented the doctrine of his opponents, but also his own. He confounds the sensitive part of our nature with the will, expressly in his definitions, though he frequently distinguishes them in his arguments. This is the reason why he sometimes asserts, that the choice of the mind is always as the sense of the most agreeable; and, at others, throws this fundamental doctrine into the form, as we have seen in our third section, that the choice of the mind is always as the choice of the mind; and holds that to deny it is a plain contradiction. By reason of the same confusion of things, the doctrine of his opponents, that "the will, in choosing, is subject to no prevailing influence," seemed to him to mean that the will, in choosing, does not choose. In both cases, he confounds the most agreeable impression upon the sensibility with the choice of the mind; and thus misrepresents both his own doctrine, and that of his opponents, by reducing the one to an insignificant truism, and the other to a glaring absurdity. President Day should have avoided the error of Edwards, in thus misconceiving the doctrine of his opponents; for he expressly distinguishes the sensibility from the will. But there is this difference between Edwards and Day; the first expressly confounds these two parts of our nature, and then proceeds to reason, in many cases, as if they were distinct; while the last most explicitly distinguishes them, and then frequently proceeds to reason as if they were one and the same. It is in this way that he also gravely teaches that the mind chooses when it chooses; and makes his adversaries assert that the mind chooses without choosing, or that the will is inclined without being inclined. Start from whatever point he will, the necessitarian never feels so strong, as when he finds himself securely intrenched in the truism, that a thing is always as itself; there manfully contending against those who assert that a thing is different from itself.

The doctrine of the liberty of indifference, as usually held, is this—that the will is not determined by any prevailing influence. This is not a perfect liberty, it is true, wherever the will is partially influenced by an extraneous cause; but it is not equivalent to the gross absurdity of the position, that the will chooses without choosing. Nor can we possibly reduce it to this form, unless we forget that the authors of it did not confound that which is supposed to exert the influence over the will, with the act of the will itself. They contended for a partial indifference of the will only; and, consequently, they could only contend for a partial, and not a perfect liberty. On the contrary, I think we should contend for a perfect indifference, not in regard to feeling, but in regard to the will. Standing on this high ground, we need not retire from the broad and open field, in order to set up the empire of a perfect liberty in a dark corner, extending to a few insignificant things only: we may establish it over the whole range of human activity, bringing out into a clear and full light, the great fact of man's perfect accountability, for all his *actions*, under all the circumstances of his life.

SECTION X.

OF ACTION AND PASSION.

THERE are no two things in nature which are more perfectly distinct than action and passion; the one necessarily excludes the other. Thus, if an effect is produced in any thing, by the action or influence of something else, then is the thing in which the effect is produced wholly passive in regard to it. The effect itself is called passion or passiveness. It is not an act of that in which it is produced; it is an effect resulting wholly from that which produces it. To say that a thing acts then, is to say that it is not passive; or, in other words, that its act is not produced by the action or influence of any thing else. To suppose that an act is so produced, is to suppose that it is not an act; the object in which it is said to be caused being wholly passive in regard to it.

If this statement be correct, it follows that an act of the mind cannot be a produced effect; that the ideas of action and passion, of cause and effect, are opposite and contrary the one to the other; and hence, it is absurd to assert that the mind may be caused to act, or that a volition can be produced by any thing acting upon the mind. This is a self-evident truth. The younger Edwards calls for proof of it; but the only evidence there is in the case, is that which arises from the nature of the things themselves, as they must appear to every mind which will bestow suitable reflection on the subject. But as he held the affirmative, maintaining that the mind is caused to act, it would have been well for him to have furnished proof himself, before he called for it from the opposite party.

It may be said, that if it were self-evident that the mind cannot be caused to act, it would appear so to all men, and there could be no doubt on the subject; that a truth or proposition cannot be said to be self-evident, unless it carries irresistible conviction to every mind to which it is proposed. But this does not follow. Previous to the time of Galileo, it was universally believed by mankind, that if a body were set in motion, it would run down of itself; though it should meet with no resistance whatever in its progress. But that great philosopher, by reflecting on the nature of matter, very clearly saw, that if a body were put in motion, and met with no resistance, it would continue to move on in a right line forever. As matter is inert, so he saw that it could not put itself in motion; and if put in motion by the action of any thing upon it, he perceived with equal clearness that it could not check itself in its career. He perceived that it is just as impossible for passive, inert matter, to change its state from motion to rest, as it is for it to change its state from rest to motion. Thus, by simply reflecting upon the nature of matter, as that which cannot act, the mind of Galileo recognized it as a self-evident and unquestionable truth, that if a body be put in motion, and there is nothing to impede its career, it will move on in a right line forever. This great law of motion, first recognized by Galileo, and afterwards adopted by all other philosophers, is called the law of inertia; because its truth necessarily results from the fact, that matter is essentially inert, or cannot act.

I am aware it has been contended by Mr. Whewell, in his Bridgewater Treatise, that the law of motion in question is not a necessary or self-evident truth; and the reason he assigns is, that if it were a truth of this nature, it would have been recognized and believed by all men before the time of Galileo. But this reason is not good. For if it did not appear self-evident to those philosophers who lived before Galileo, it was because they did not bestow sufficient reflection upon the subject, and not because it was not a self-evident truth. All men had seen bodies moving only in a resisting medium, amid counteracting influences; and having always seen them run down in such a medium, they very naturally concluded that a body put in motion would run down of itself. Yielding to an illusion of the senses, instead of rising above it by a sustained effort of reason and meditation, they supposed that the motion of a body would spend itself in the course of time, and so come to an end without any cause of its extinction. This is the reason why they did not see, what must have appeared to be a self-evident truth, if they had bestowed sufficient reflection upon the subject, instead of being swayed by an illusion of the senses.

Mr. Whewell admits the law in question to be a truth; he only denies that it is a necessary or self-evident truth. Now, if it be not a necessary truth, I should like to know how he has ascertained it to be a truth at all. Has any man ever seen a body put in motion, and continue to move on in a right line forever? Has any man ever ascertained the truth of this law by observation and experiment? It is evident, that if it be true at all, it must be a necessary truth. Who that is capable of rising above the associations of sense, so as to view things as they are in themselves, can meditate upon this subject, without perceiving that the law of *inertia* is a self-evident truth, necessarily arising out of the very nature of matter?

It does not follow, then, that a truth is not "self-evident", because it does not appear so to all men; for some may be blinded to the truth by an illusion of the senses. This is the case, with the necessitarian. He has always seen the motion of body produced by the action of something else; and hence, confounding the activity of mind with the motion of body, he concludes that volition is produced by the prior action of something else. All that he needs in order to see the impossibility of such a thing, is severe and sustained meditation. But how can we expect this from him? Is he not a great reasoner, rather than a great thinker? Does he not display his skill in drawing logical conclusions from the illusions of the senses, and assumptions founded thereon; rather than in laying his foundations and his premises aright, in the immutable depths of meditation and consciousness? We may appeal to his *reason*, and he will fall to *reasoning*. We may ask for *meditation*, and he will give us *logic*. Indeed, he wants that severe and scrutinizing observation which pierces through all the illusions and associations of the senses, rising to a contemplation of things as they are in themselves; which is one of the best attributes of the great thinker.

To show that he does this, I shall begin with President Day. No other necessitarian has made so formal and elaborate an attempt to prove, that the mind may be caused to act. He undertakes to answer the objection which has been urged against the scheme of moral necessity, that it confounds action and passion. It is alleged, that a volition cannot be produced or caused by the action or influence of any thing. To this President Day replies, "these are terms of very convenient ambiguity, with which it is easy to construct a plausible but fallacious argument. The word passive is sometimes used to signify that which is *inactive*. With this meaning, it must, of course, be the opposite of every thing which is active. To say that that which is in *this* sense passive, is at the same time active, is to assert that that which is active is not active. But this is not the only signification of the term passive in common use. It is very frequently used to express the relation of an effect to its cause," p. 159.

Now, here is the distinction, but is it not without a difference? If an effect is produced, is it not passive in relation to its cause? This is not denied. Is it active then in relation to any thing? President Day says it is. But is this so? Is not an effect, which is wholly produced in one thing by the action or influence of another, wholly passive? Is not the thing which, according to the supposition, is wholly passive to the influence acting upon it, wholly passive? In other words; is it made to act? Does it not merely suffer? If it is endued with an active nature, and really puts forth an act, is not this act clearly different from the passive impression made upon it?

One would certainly suppose so, but for the logic of the necessitarian. Let us examine this logic. "The term passive," says President Day, "is sometimes employed to express the relation of an effect to its cause. In this sense, it is so far from being inconsistent with activity, that activity may be the very effect which is produced. A thing may be *caused* to be active. A cannon shot is said to be passive, with respect to the charge of powder which impels it. But is there no activity given to the ball? Is not the whirlwind active, when it tears up the forest?" &c. &c., p. 160.

Now, all these illustrations are brought to show that the mind may be caused to act;—that it may be passive in relation to the cause of its volition, and active in relation to the effect of its volition. A more striking instance could not be adduced to prove the correctness of the assertion already made, that the necessitarian confounds the motion of body with the action of mind. "A thing may be caused to act," says President Day. But how does he show this? By showing that a thing may be caused to move! "Is no *activity* given to the ball? Is not the whirlwind *active*, when it tears up the forest?" And so he goes on, leaving the light of reason and of consciousness; now rushing into the darkness of the whirlwind; now riding "on the mountain wave;" and now plunging into the depths of "volcanic lava;"—all the time in quest of light respecting the phenomena of mind! We could have wished him to stop awhile, in the impetuous current of rhetoric, and inform us, whether he really considers, "the motion of a ball" as the same thing with the volition of the mind. If he does, then he may suppose that his illustrations are to the purpose, how great soever may be his mistake; but if he supposes there is a real difference between them, how can he ever pretend to show that mind may be caused to act, by showing that body may be caused to move?

I freely admit, that body may be caused to move. Body is perfectly passive in motion; and hence, its motion may be caused. But the mind is not passive in volition; and hence the difference in the two cases. It is an error, as I have already said, pervading the views of the necessitarian, that he confounds the action of mind with the motion of body. Even Mr. Locke, who, in some places, has recognized the essential difference between them, has frequently confounded them in his reasonings and illustrations. Hence, it becomes necessary to bear this distinction always in mind, in the examination of their writings. It should be rendered perfectly clear to our minds by meditation; and never permitted to grow dim through forgetfulness. This is indispensably necessary to shut out the illusions of the senses, in order that we may have a clear and unclouded view of the phenomena of nature.

Is the motion of body, then, one and the same thing with the action of mind? They are frequently called by the same name. The motion of mind, and the action of body, are very common modes of expression. Body is said to act, when it only moves; and mind is said to move, when it really acts. These metaphors and supposed analogies are intimately and inseparably interwoven into the very frame-work of our language; and hence the necessity of guarding against them in our conceptions. They are almost as subtle as the great adversary of truth; and therefore we should be constantly on the watch, lest we should be deceived or misled by them.

Let us look, then, at these things just as they are in themselves. When a body moves, it simply passes from one place to another; and when the mind acts or chooses, it simply prefers one thing to another. Here, there is no real identity or sameness of nature. The body *suffers* a change; the mind itself *acts*. The one is pure passim or passiveness; the other is pure action—the very opposite of passivity. The one is a *suffering*, and the other is a *doing*. There are no two things in the whole range of nature, which are more perfectly and essentially distinct; and he who confounds them in his reasonings, as philosophers have so often done, can never arrive at a clear perception of the truth.

President Day, if he intended any thing to the purpose, undertook to show that an act may be produced in mind, in that which is active, by the action or influence of something else; and what has he shown? Why, that body may be caused to move! Let a case be produced in which the mind, the active soul of man, is made to act: let a case be produced in which a volition is caused to exist in the soul of man, by the action or influence of any thing whatever, and it will be something to the purpose: but what does it signify to tell us, that a body, that that which is wholly and essentially passive in its nature, may be made to move, or *suffer* a change of place? A more palpable sophism was never perpetrated; and that such a mind should have recourse to such an argument, only betrays the miserable weakness, and the forlorn hopelessness, of the cause in which it is enlisted.

Indeed, the learned president seems, after all, to be at least half conscious that the analogies of matter can throw no light on the phenomena of mind; and that what he has so eloquently said, amounts to just nothing at all. For he says, "It may be objected, that these are all examples of *inanimate* objects; and that they have no proper application to mental activity," p. 161. Yes, truly, this is the very objection which we should urge against all the fine illustrations of President Day; and it is a full and complete answer to them. It is the great principle of the inductive study of mind, that its phenomena can be understood only in so far as we have observed them in the pure light of consciousness, and no farther; they should never be viewed through the darkening and confounding analogies of matter.

No one, that I know of, has ever denied that a body may be caused to move; the only point on which we desire to be enlightened is, whether the mind may be caused to act. To this point President Day next directly comes.

71

Leaving "inanimate objects," he says, "take the case of deep and earnest thinking. Is there no activity in this? And is it without a cause? When reading the orations of Demosthenes, or the demonstrations of Newton, are our minds wholly inactive; or if they think intensely, have our thoughts no dependence on the book before us?" p. 161. Truly, there is activity in this, in our "deep and earnest thinking"; but what is the cause of this activity? Does the book before us *cause* us to think? This is the point at which the argument of the author is driving, and to which it should come, if it would be to the purpose, and yet he does not seem to like to speak it out right manfully; and hence, instead of saying that the book causes us to think, he chooses to say that our thoughts have a *dependence* on the book. It is true, that no man can read a book, unless he has it to read; and, consequently, his thoughts in reading the book are absolutely dependent on the possession of it. But still, the possession of a book is the *condition*, and not the *cause*, of his reading it. The cause of a thing, and the indispensable *condition* of it, are perfectly distinct from each other; and the argument of Day, in confounding them, has presented us with another sophism.

The ideas of a condition and of a cause, though so different in themselves, are always blended together by necessitarians; and hence the confusion into which they run. Edwards has united them, as we have seen, under the term cause; and then employed this term to signify the one or the other at his pleasure. The word "dependence," is the favourite of President Day; and he uses it with fully as much vagueness and vacillation of meaning, as Edwards does the term cause. He has undertaken to show us, that the mind may be *caused* to act; and he has shown us, that a particular class of thoughts cannot come to existence, except upon a particular condition! This is not to reason; but to slip and to slide from one meaning of an ambiguous word to another.

When it is said that the mind cannot be caused to act, President Day must have known in what sense the term cause is used in this proposition. He must have known, that no one meant to assert, that there are no *conditions* or *antecedents*, on which the action of the mind depends. There is not an advocate of free-agency in the universe, who will contend, that the mind can choose a thing, unless there is a thing to be chosen; or, to take his own illustration, can read a book, unless there is a book to be read. The question is not, whether there are *conditions*, without the existence of which the mind cannot act; this no one denies; but whether there is, or can be, a real and efficient cause of the mind's action. The point in dispute, relates not to mere fact of dependence, but to the *nature* of that dependence. The question is, *can the mind be efficiently caused to act?* This being the question, what does it signify to tell us, that it cannot read a book, unless it has a book to read? Or what does it signify to tell us, that a body may be caused to move? These are mere irrelevancies; they fall short of the point in dispute; and they only seem to reach it by means of a very "convenient ambiguity" of words.

But still it may be said, that although a body is passive in motion, it may act upon other bodies, and thereby communicate motion to them. This is the ground taken by President Day. "The very same thing," says he, "may be both cause and effect. The mountain wave, which is the effect of the wind, may be the cause which buries the ship in the ocean," p. 160. I am aware, that one body is frequently said to *act* upon another; but this word action, as President Day has well said, is a term "of very convenient ambiguity, with which it is easy to construct a plausible but fallacious argument," p. 159. The only cause in every case of motion, is that *force*, whatever it may be, which acts upon the body moved, and puts it in motion. All the rest is pure passion or passiveness. The motion of the body is not action; it is the most pure passion of which the mind can form a conception. If a body in action is said to act upon another, this is but a metaphor; there is no real action in the case. Indeed, if a body be put in motion, and meets with no resistance, it will move on in a right line forever—and why? just because of its *inertia*, of its inherent destitution of a power to act. As a mathematician, President Day certainly knew all this; but he seems to have forgotten it all, in his eagerness to support the cause of moral necessity.

He saw that motion is frequently called action; he saw that one body is sometimes said to act upon another; and this was sufficient for his purpose. He did not reflect upon the natures of motion and of volition, as they are in themselves; he views them through the medium of an ambiguous phraseology. Nor did he reflect, that if motion is communicated from one body to another, this is not because one body really acts upon another, but because it is impossible for two bodies to occupy the same place at one and the same time. He did not reflect, that if motion is communicated from one body to another, this does not arise from the activity, but from the impenetrability of matter. In short, he did not reflect, that there is no state or phenomena of matter, whatever may be its name, that at all resembles the state of mind which we call action or volition; or else he would have seen, that all his illustrations drawn from material objects can throw no light on the point in controversy.

We find the same confusion of things in the works of the Edwardses. We do not at all confound action and passion, President Edwards contends, by supposing that acts of the soul are effects, wherein the soul is the object of something acting upon and influencing it, p. 203. And again, "It is no more a contradiction to suppose that action may be the effect of some other cause beside the agent, or being that acts, than to suppose that life may be the effect of some other cause beside the being that lives," p. 203. The younger Edwards also asserts, that "to say that an agent that is acted upon cannot act, is as groundless, as to say, that a body acted upon cannot move," p. 131. We might adduce many similar passages; but these are sufficient. What do they prove? If they are any thing to the purpose, they are only so by confounding motion with volition, passion with action.

No one would pretend to deny, that the mind may be, and is, caused to exist, or that the agent may be caused to live. In regard to our being and living we are perfectly passive; and hence we admit that we may be caused to exist and to live. *Living* and *being* are not *acting*. We are not passive in regard to volition; this is an act of the mind itself. The above assertions only overlook the slight circumstance that *being* and *doing* are two different things; that motion is not volition, that passion is not action. This strange confusion of things is very common in the writings of the Edwardses, as well as in those of all other necessitarians.

Edwards held volition to be a produced effect. This identifies a passive impression made upon the mind, with an act of the mind itself. In order to escape this difficulty, Edwards was bound to show that action and passion are not opposite in their natures. "Action, when properly set in opposition to passion or passiveness," says he, "is no real existence; it is not the same with *an action*, but is a mere relation." And again, "Action and passion are not two contrary natures;" when placed in opposition they are only contrary relations. The same ground is taken by President Day. "Are not cause and effect," says he, "opposite in their natures? They are opposite relations, but not always opposite things." They contend, that an object may be passive in relation to one thing, and active in relation to another; that a volition may be passive in relation to its producing cause, and yet active in relation to its produced effect.

Now, this is not true. An act is opposite in its nature to a passive impression made upon the mind. This every man may clearly see by suitable reflection, if he will not blind himself to the truth, as the necessitarian always does, by false analogies drawn from the world of matter, and the phenomena of motion. We have seen how President Day has attempted to show, that an object may be passive in relation to one thing, and yet active in relation to another; and that in all these attempts he has confounded the motion of body with the action or choice of mind. We have seen that all the illustrations adduced to throw light on this subject are fallacious. Let this subject be studied in the light of consciousness, not through the darkening and confounding medium of false analogies, and we may safely anticipate a verdict in our favour. For who that will closely and steadily reflect upon *an action* of the mind, does not perceive that it is different, in nature and in kind, from a passive impression made upon the mind from without? I do not say action, which President Edwards seems to think does not signify any thing positive, such as *an action*, when it is set in opposition to passion; but I say that *an action* itself is opposite in its nature to passion, to a produced effect.

President Edwards cannot escape the absurdity of his doctrine by alleging, that when action and passion are set in opposition, they do not signify opposite natures, but only opposite relations. For he has confounded *an act* of the mind with a *passive impression* made thereon; and these things are opposite in their natures, whether he is pleased to say that action and passion are opposite *natures* or not.

This position may be easily established. "I humbly conceive," says he, "that the affections of the soul are not properly distinguished from the will, as though they were two faculties in the soul." ... . "The affections are no other than the more vigorous and sensible exercises of the inclination and will of the soul." These passages are referred to by President Day to prove, that Edwards regarded our "emotions or affections as acts of the will," p. 39. Having confounded the will and the sensibility, it became exceedingly easy for Edwards to show that a volition may be produced or caused: all that he had to do was to show, that an emotion may be produced, which is the same thing with an act of the will or a volition. It is upon this confusion of things, that his whole system rests; for if the sensibility is different from the will, as most persons, at the present day, will admit it is; then to excite an emotion, or to make a passive impression upon the sensibility, is very different from producing a volition.

Edwards has taken great pains with the superstructure of his system, while he has left its foundations without support. He has not shown, nor can any man show, that the sensibility and the will are one and the same faculty of the soul. He assumes that an emotion is an act of the will, and then proceeds to build upon it, and to argue from it, as if it were a clear and unquestionable truth. Thus, he repeatedly says, that whatever pleases us most, or excites the most agreeable sensation, is that which "operates to induce a volition;" and to say otherwise, is to assert that that which pleases us most, does not please us most. Such assertions, (and I have already had occasion to adduce many such,) clearly identify a sense of the most agreeable, or the most pleasing emotion, with an act of the will. His definition, as we have already seen, laid the foundation for this, and his arguments are based upon it. The passive impression, or the sensation produced, is, according to Edwards, a volition! No wonder, then, that he could conceive of an action of the mind *as being produced*. The wonder is, how he could conceive of it *as being an action at all*.

Let us suppose, now, that a feeling or an emotion is produced by an object in view of the mind. It will follow, that the mind is passive in feeling, or in experiencing emotion. We are conscious of such feeling or emotion; and hence we infer, that we are susceptible of feeling or emotion. This susceptibility we call the sensibility, the heart, the affections, &c. But there is another phenomenon of our nature, which is perfectly distinct in nature and in kind from an emotion or a feeling. We are conscious of a volition or choice; and hence we infer that we have a power of acting, or putting forth volitions. This power we call the will.

Now, the phenomena exhibited by these two faculties of the soul, the sensibility and the will, are entirely different from each other; and there is not the least shadow of evidence going to show that the faculties themselves are one and the same. On the contrary, we are compelled by a fundamental law of belief, to regard the susceptibility of our nature, by which we feel, as different from that power of the soul, by which we act or put forth volitions. The only reason we have for saying that matter is different from mind, is that its manifestations or phenomena are different; and we have a similar reason for asserting, that the emotive part of our nature, or the sensibility, is distinct from the will. And yet, in the face of all this, President Edwards has expressly denied that there is any difference between these two faculties of the soul. It is in this confusion of things, in this false psychology, that he has laid the foundation of his system.

If President Edwards be right, it is no wonder that the younger Edwards should so often assert, that it is no more absurd to say, that volition may be caused, than it is to say, that feeling or emotion may be caused. For, if the doctrine in question be true, a volition is an emotion or feeling; and to produce the one is to produce the other. How short and easy has the path of the necessitarian been made, by a convenient definition!

If we only bear the distinction between the sensibility and the will in mind, it will be exceedingly easy to see through the cloudy sophistications of the necessitarian. "How does it appear to be a *fact*," asks President Day, "that the will cannot act when it is acted upon?" I reply that the *will* is not acted upon at all; that passive impressions are made upon the sensibility, and not upon the will. This is a *fact* which the necessitarian always overlooks.

Again; the same object may be both passive and active; passive with respect to one thing, and active with respect to another. Thus, says President Day, "The axe is passive, with respect to the hand which moves it; but active, with respect to the object which it strikes. The cricket club is passive in *receiving* motion from the hand of the player; it is active in *communicating* motion to the ball." The fallacy of all such illustrations, in confounding motion and action, I have already noticed, and I intend to say nothing more in relation to this point. But there is another less palpable fallacy in them.

How are such illustrations intended to be applied to the phenomena of volition? Is it meant, that volition itself is passive in relation to one thing, and active in relation to another? If so, I reply it is absurd to affirm, that volition, or an act, is passive in relation to any thing? Is it meant, that not volition itself, but the will, is passive to that which acts upon it, while it is active in relation to its effect? If so, I contend that the will is not acted upon at all; that the passive impression is made upon the sensibility, and not upon the will. Is it supposed, that it is neither the volition nor the will, which is both active and passive at the same time; but that it is the mind? This may be very true. The mind may be passive, if you please, in relation to that which acts upon its sensibility, while it is active in volition; but how does this prove the doctrine, that *an act* may be produced by something else acting upon the will? How does this show, that action and passion are not confounded, in supposing that an act is caused? The passive impression, the state of the sensibility is produced but this is not *a volition*. The passive impression exists in the sensibility; the volition exists in the will. The first is a produced effect; the last is an act of the mind. And the only way in which this act of the mind itself has been linked with that which acts upon the mind, as an effect is linked with its cause, has been by confounding the *sensibility* with the *will*; and the light of this distinction is no sooner held up, than we see that a very important link is wanting in the chain of the necessitarian's logic. Let this light be carried around through all the dark corners of his system, and through all its dark labyrinths of words; and many a lurking sophism will be detected and brought out from its unsuspected hiding place.

When it is said, that the same thing may be active and passive, this remark should be understood with reference to the mind itself. The language of the necessitarian, I am aware, sometimes points to the volition itself, and sometimes to the will; but we should always understand him as referring to the mind. He may not have so understood himself; but he must be so understood. For it is not the will that acts; it is the mind. This is conceded by the necessitarian. Hence, when he says, that the same thing may be both active and passive, he must be understood as applying this proposition to the mind itself; and not to the will or to volition. It is the mind that acts; and hence the mind must be also passive; or we cannot say that *the same thing* may be both active and passive.

The mind then, it may be said, is both active and passive at the same time. But it is passive in regard to its emotions and feelings; and hence, if you please, these may be produced. It is active in regard to its volitions, or rather in its volitions; and hence these cannot be produced by the action of any thing upon the mind. To show that they can, the necessitarian, as we have seen, has confounded a passive impression with an active volition. If these be distinct, as they most clearly are, the necessitarian can make his point good, only by showing that the passive impression made upon the mind, is connected with the volition of the mind, as a producing cause is connected with its effect. But this he has not shown; and hence his whole system rests upon gratuitous and unfounded assumptions. I say his whole system; for if the mind cannot be caused to act, if it is absurd to speak of a produced action, it is not true, that an action or volition does or can result from the necessitating action, or influence of motives.

SECTION XI.

OF THE ARGUMENT FROM THE FOREKNOWLEDGE OF GOD.

THE argument from the foreknowledge of God, is one on which the necessitarian relies with great confidence. Nor is this at all surprising; since to so many minds, even among distinguished philosophers, the prescience of Deity and the free-agency of man have appeared to be irreconcilable.

Thus, says Mr. Stewart, "I have mentioned the attempt of Clarke and others to show that no valid argument against the scheme of free-will can be deduced from the prescience of God, even supposing *that* to extend to all the actions of voluntary beings. On this point I must decline offering any opinion of my own, because I conceive it as placed far beyond the reach of our faculties." Dr. Campbell also says, "To reconcile the divine prescience with the freedom, and even contingency, and consequently with the good or ill desert of human actions, is what I have never yet seen achieved by any, and indeed despair of seeing." And Mr. Locke declares, "I cannot make freedom in man consistent with omnipotence and omniscience in God, though I am as fully persuaded of both as of any truth I most firmly assent to; and therefore I have long since given off the consideration of that subject, resolving all into this short conclusion, that if it is possible for God to make a free-agent, then man is free, though I see not the way of it."

Sentiments like these, which are so often met with in the writings of eminent philosophers, have repeatedly led me to reconsider the conclusion at which I have arrived on this subject; but I have been able to discover no reason why it should be abandoned. Indeed, if authority were a sufficient reason why the great difficulty in question should be regarded as incapable of being solved, I should abandon it in despair, and leave the necessitarian to make the most of his argument; but it has only induced me to proceed with the greater caution; and this, instead of having shaken my convictions, has settled them with the greater firmness and clearness in my mind. Whether I am in the right, or whether I labour under a hallucination, satisfactory only to myself, and perplexing to all others, I must submit to the candid consideration of the reader.

Why should it be thought impossible to reconcile the free-agency of man with the foreknowledge of God? No one pretends that there is any disagreement between the things themselves, as they really exist; if there is any discrepancy in the case, it must exist only between our ideas of foreknowledge and free-agency. Indeed, we cannot think of the things themselves, or compare them, except by means of the ideas we have formed of then; and if our ideas of them are really irreconcilable, it is because they have not been correctly formed, and do not correspond with the things themselves. What shall we do then? Shall we set to work to reform our ideas? Shall we explain away the free-agency of man, or deny the foreknowledge of God? No. We may retain both.

Edwards contends, that volitions are brought to pass by the influence of motives, and that it is impossible in any case, that a volition should depart from the influence of the strongest motive. This is the great doctrine of moral necessity, which it is the object of President Edwards to establish. Now, if his celebrated argument, or "demonstration," as it is called, proves this point, then it is to be held as true and valid; but if it only proves some other thing which is called by the name of necessity, it is not to the purpose. And if it can be shown, that his argument does not prove any thing at all in relation to the causation of choice, it will appear that it has no relevancy to the point at issue.

The foreknowledge of God, I admit, infers the necessity of all human actions, in one sense of the word; but not that *kind* of necessity for which any necessitarian pleads, or against which *any* libertarian is at all concerned to contend. The fallacy of the argument in question is, that it shows all human actions to be necessary in a sense in which it is not opposed to any scheme of liberty whatever, and assumes them to be necessary in another and quite different sense; and thus the great doctrine of freewill, otherwise so clear and unquestionable, is overshadowed and obscured by an imperfect and ambiguous phraseology, rather than by the inherent difficulties of the subject. This is the position which I shall endeavour to establish.

The first argument of President Edwards is as follows. When the existence of a thing is infallibly and indissolubly connected with something else, which has already had existence, then its existence is necessary; but the future volitions of moral agents, are infallibly and indissolubly connected with the foreknowledge of God; and therefore they are necessary, p. 114-15. Now this argument is perfectly sound; the conclusion is really contained in the premise, or definition of necessity, and it is fairly deduced from it. It is as perfect as any syllogism in Euclid *but what does it prove?* It proves that all human actions are necessary—but in what sense? Does it prove that they are necessary with a *moral necessity?* Does it prove that they are brought to pass by the influence of moral causes? No such thing is even pretended: "I allow what Dr. Whitby says to be true," says Edwards, "that mere foreknowledge does not affect the thing known, to *make* it more certain or future," p. 122. He admits that foreknowledge exerts "no influence on the thing known to make it necessary." He does not even pretend that there is any *moral necessity* shown to exist by this argument; and hence his conclusion has no connexion with the great doctrine of the Inquiry, or the point in dispute. It aims at the word, but not at the thing. The infallible connexion it shows to exist, is admitted to be entirely different from the infallible connexion between moral causes and volitions; that is to say, it is admitted that it does not prove any thing to the purpose.

But is the indissoluble connexion, or necessity, established by this argument, at all inconsistent with human liberty? If it is not; and if our scheme of liberty is perfectly consistent and reconcilable with it; then it infers nothing, and is nothing, that is opposed to what we hold.

This question admits of an easy solution. The foreknowledge of a future event proves it to be necessary in precisely the same manner that the knowledge of a present event shows it to be necessary. This is conceded by Edwards. "All certain knowledge," says he, "whether it be foreknowledge, or after knowledge, or concomitant knowledge, proves the thing known now to be necessary, by some means or other; *or proves that it is impossible it should now be otherwise than true*," p. 121. And again, "All certain knowledge proves the necessity of the truth known; whether it be *before*, or *after*, or *at the same time*," p. 124; and so in other places.

In what sense then, let us inquire, does the knowledge of a present event prove it to be necessary? It is necessary, says Edwards, because it is indissolubly connected with the knowledge of it. In other words, it could not possibly be known to exist, unless it did exist; and hence, its existence is said to be indissolubly connected with the knowledge of its existence, or, in other words, it is said to be necessary. This is all true; but is this indissoluble connexion, or necessity, at all inconsistent with the contingency of the event known? *This is the question;* and let us not lose sight of it in a mist of words. Let it be distinctly borne in mind, and it will be easily settled.

For this purpose, let us suppose, to adopt the language of President Edwards, "that nonentity is about to bring forth;" and that an event comes into being without any cause of its existence. This event then exists; it is seen, and it is known to exist. Now, even on this wild supposition, there is an infallible and indissoluble connexion between the existence of the event and the knowledge of it; and hence it is necessary, in the sense above explained. But what has this necessary connexion to do with the cause of its existence? This indissoluble connexion, this dire necessity, is perfectly consistent, as we have seen, with the supposition that the event had no cause at all of its existence. How can it conflict, then, with any scheme of free-agency that ever was dreamed of by man?

If this argument proves any thing in regard to human actions, it only proves that a volition has an effect, and not that it has a cause. Indeed, it has been said, that the knowledge of an event is the effect of its existence; and the same remark has been extended to the foreknowledge of God with respect to the future volitions of human beings. This position is not denied by Edwards; he considers, in fact, that it strengthens, rather than weakens, his argument. "Because it shows the existence of the event to be so settled and firm, that *it is as if it had already been;* inasmuch as *in effect* it actually exists already;" and much more to the same purpose, p.122-3. "It is as strong arguing," says he, "from the effect to the cause, as from the cause to the effect."

This is all true; it is as strong arguing from effect to cause, as it is from cause to effect. But do the arguments prove the same thing? Let us see. I know a thing to exist; and therefore it does exist. This is to reason from effect to cause. The conclusion is inevitable; but what does it prove? Why, it proves that the thing does exist—it proves the bare fact of existence. The indissoluble connexion, or the necessity, in this case, exists between the knowledge and the event known; and it has no relation to the question how the event came to exist. This argument, then, in regard to human volitions, only proves that they are indissolubly connected with their effects, and are necessarily implied by them; just as every cause is implied by its effects: but no libertarian in the world has ever questioned such a position. For all that such an argument proves, all the volitions of moral agents may come into existence, without having the least shadow of reason or ground of their existence. We admit that volitions are efficient causes; and that they have effects, with which they are indissolubly connected. Edwards undertook to show, that volitions are necessary, because they are infallibly and indissolubly connected with their causes; and he has shown that they are necessary, because they are infallibly and indissolubly connected with their effects! This is one branch of his great argument.

There is another sense, in which the knowledge of an event, whether it be *fore*, or *after*, or *concomitant*, knowledge, proves it to be necessary. This sense is not clearly distinguished from the former by Edwards. He recognizes them both, however, although he blends them together, and frequently turns from the one to the other in the course of his argument. It is highly important, and affords no little satisfaction, to keep them clearly distinct in our minds.

A thing is said to be necessary, as we have seen, because it is connected with the knowledge of it; and, if a thing does exist, or is certainly and infallibly known to exist, it may be said to be necessary, on the principle that it is impossible it should exist and not exist at one and the same time. These two things are evidently different; and, for the sake of distinctness in our language, as well as in our thoughts, I shall call the first a *logical*, and the last an *axiomatical* necessity. A thing, then, which does exist, is said to be necessary with an *axiomatical* necessity; because it is impossible for it not to exist while it does exist: and it is said to be necessary, with a *logical* necessity, because it is indissolubly connected with the knowledge of it. The former kind of necessity is frequently presented in this form of expression, that if a thing does exist, it is impossible it should be otherwise than true that it does exist. In this form of expression, it is frequently resorted to by Edwards.

Thus, says he, "I observed before, in explaining the nature of necessity, that in things which are past, their past existence is now *necessary;* having already made sure of existence, *it is now impossible that it should be otherwise than true, that the thing has existed,*" p. 114-15. Just so we may say in relation to things which now exist; for, having already made sure of existence, it is impossible it should be otherwise than true, that they do now exist; or, in other words, it is impossible they should not exist while they do exist. In like manner, if the future existence of any thing is foreknown, "it is impossible it should be otherwise than true," that it should exist, or come to pass: that is to say, if it will exist, it will be impossible for it not to exist at the time of its existence.

Foreknowledge, I admit, infers this kind of necessity; but is this any thing to the purpose? The conclusion is the same, whether it be deduced from foreknowledge, or concomitant knowledge. Let us suppose, then, for the sake of clearness and convenience, that a thing is now known to exist. It follows from hence, by a *logical* necessity, that it does exist; for it could not possibly be known to exist, unless it did exist. And, as it does exist, "it is impossible that it should be otherwise than true that it does exist;" or, in other words, it is impossible for it not to exist now, while it does exist. This is all there is in this part of the argument.

And what does it amount to? It is a simple declaration of what no body ever denied—that if a thing exists, or is to exist, or has existed, it is impossible to conceive of it as not existing at the time of its existence. All this is perfectly true, without the least reference to the question, how it came to exist, or how it will come to exist? It is wholly irrelevant to the point at issue. It controverts no position, held by any sane man that now lives, or that ever has lived.

In other words, if a thing is known to exist, certainly and infallibly, then it does exist; and if it does exist, then "it is impossible it should be otherwise than true" that it does exist; and hence its existence is said to be necessary with an *axiomatical* necessity. But this does not prove that it is *necessarily produced*. For, supposing it to exist, its existence would be necessary in the above sense, even if it had no cause of its existence. The necessity here referred to, is a necessity *in the order of our ideas*, and not *in the course of events*. It arises from the impossibility of a thing's not existing at the time it does exist; and it has no reference whatever to the causation of any thing: it is a fundamental law of belief, and not a *causal* necessity. These three things, an *axiomatical*, a *logical*, and a *causal* necessity, are most strangely confounded in the argument of President Edwards.

Will it be said, that in this argument, it was not the object of Edwards, to prove that there is a moral necessity in regard to our volitions; but only that they are "not without all necessity?" Suppose this to be the case, with whom has he any controversy, or to what purpose has he argued? No one has ever held that human volitions are "without all necessity," according to Edwards' use of that term; and no one can hold it. No one can deny, that there is an indissoluble connexion between the existence of a thing, and the certain and infallible knowledge of its existence; or between the effect of a thing and the thing itself; or that it is impossible for a thing not to exist while it does exist. In these senses of the word, all rational creatures are bound to acknowledge that human volitions are necessary. The most strenuous advocate of free-agency has not one word to say against them; and such being the meaning of Edwards, we must all heartily concur with him, when he says, "that there is no geometrical theorem or proposition whatever more capable of *strict demonstration*, than that God's certain prescience of the volition of moral agents is inconsistent with such a contingency of these events, *as is without all necessity*," p. 125-6.

If it can be truly said, that a thing is foreknown, it follows that it will come to pass, or the proposition which affirms the future existence of it, is necessarily true. In other words, it is self-contradictory and absurd, to assert that a thing is foreknown, and yet that it may not come to pass; just as it is to assert that a thing is known to exist and yet at the same time does not exist. Hence, it is frequently alleged by Edwards, that to deny his conclusions, drawn from foreknowledge, is self-contradictory and absurd; unless we deny foreknowledge itself. To admit this, says he, and yet contend that the thing foreknown may possibly not be, is to fall into a plain contradiction, and "to suppose God's foreknowledge to be inconsistent with itself," p. 117. Is it not strange, that it did not occur to Edwards, that if to deny his position is to deny that God foreknows what he foreknows; then to affirm it, is only to affirm that he foreknows what he foreknows? Indeed, all those reasonings in which he represents the denial of his position as self-contradictory and absurd, should have convinced him that he could prove nothing to the purpose, by arguing from the foreknowledge of God, or else he must assume the very thing in dispute, by taking it for granted that it is future; or, which is the same thing in effect, that it is foreknown. For in admitting any premise, we admit, no more than is contained in it; and if we only deny what is not contained in our admission, we are not involved in a self-contradiction, or absurdity. In alleging that we have done this, therefore, in the present case;—in alleging that we contradict ourselves by admitting the foreknowledge of God, and in denying necessity, he takes it for granted that the very thing in dispute is included in that foreknowledge. In other words, if Edwards does not mean to say, that the point in dispute is included in the foreknowledge of God; then he cannot say, that we contradict ourselves by admitting that divine prescience; and if he does mean to say, that the thing which we deny is included in the foreknowledge of God, then he begs the question.

It is freely conceded, that whatever God foreknows will most certainly and infallibly come to pass. He foresees all human volitions; and, therefore, they will most certainly and infallibly come to pass, in some manner or other: the bare fact of their future existence is clearly established by God's foreknowledge of them. And if all human volitions will be brought to pass, by the operation of moral causes; then this manner of their existence is foreknown to God, and will all come to pass in this way; but to take this for granted, is to beg the question. We have just as much right to suppose, that God foreknows that the volitions of moral agents are not necessitated, as the necessitarian has to suppose that He foreknows the contrary; and then it would follow that our volitions are necessarily free, or without any producing causes. If God foreknows that our actions will come to pass in the way we call freely, (and we have as much right to this supposition as our opponents have to the contrary,) then, as foreknowledge infers necessity, our actions are necessarily free. And surely, if the necessity which is inferred from foreknowledge, is predicable of freedom itself, it cannot be inconsistent with it.

In other words, if the necessity of human volitions, according to the scheme of Edwards, be a fact, then it was foreknown to God that such is the fact; and, if we please, we may infer the fact from his foreknowledge, after having inferred his foreknowledge from the fact. On the other hand, if the scheme of necessity be a mere hypothesis, having no corresponding reality in the universe; then God never foreknew that it is according to such scheme that all human actions are brought to pass; unless he foreknew things to be necessitated which in reality are not necessitated. Hence, we can prove nothing by reasoning from the foreknowledge of God; except what we first assume to be true, and consequently foreknown to Him; and, if we choose to resort to this pitiful way of begging the question, we may prove our hypothesis just as well as any other.

The foreknowledge of an event, as I have already said, proves nothing more nor less than *the bare certainty* of its future existence; it decides nothing as *to the manner* of its coming into existence. The necessitarian may ring the changes upon this subject as long as he pleases, and all he can possibly make out of it is, that if God foreknows a thing, it will certainly be, and to suppose otherwise, is a contradiction. Thus, says Edwards, "To suppose the future volitions of moral agents not to be necessary events; or, which is the same thing, events which it is not possible but that they may come to pass; and yet to suppose that God certainly foreknows them, and knows all things, is to suppose God's knowledge to be inconsistent with itself. For to say that God certainly, and without all conjecture, knows that a thing will infallibly be, which at the same time he knows to be so *contingent* that it may possibly not be, is to suppose his knowledge inconsistent with itself; or that one thing he knows is utterly inconsistent with another thing he knows. It is the same as to say, he now knows a proposition to be of certain infallible truth, which he knows to be of contingent uncertain truth. If a future volition is so without all necessity, that nothing hinders but it may not be, then the proposition which asserts its future existence is so uncertain, that nothing hinders but that the truth of it may entirely fail. And if God knows all things, he knows this proposition to be thus uncertain; and that is inconsistent with his knowing it to be infallibly true; and so inconsistent with his knowing that it is true." p. 117. Now all this going around and around amounts to just this, that if God certainly and infallibly foreknows a thing, he certainly and infallibly foreknows it, or that if it will certainly come to pass, it will certainly come to pass.

We admit that the certainty of all future events is implied in God's foreknowledge of them. Does the argument in question prove any more than the bare fact of the certainty of the events foreknown? The argument, so far as we have yet followed it, clearly does not. It merely proves the bare fact of the certainty of existence. Indeed, Edwards himself says, that "metaphysical or philosophical necessity," (and this is the necessity for which he here contends,) "is nothing different from their certainty." p. 23. And the younger Edwards frequently says, "If a proposition asserting some future event, be a real and absolute truth, there is an absolute certainty of the event; *such absolute certainty is all that is implied in the divine foreknowledge; and all the moral necessity for which we plead.*" p. 160. Now, if these writers merely mean that a thing is certain, when they say it is necessary, it is to be regretted that they did not use the right word. It would have saved their works from no little confusion.

But the truth is, that the moral necessity for which they contend consists sometimes in the certainty of an event, and sometimes in *the ground* of that certainty. Volitions are said to be morally necessitory in their definition, and in their system, because they are *made certain by the influence of moral causes.* But in their arguments, and the defence of their system, *the bare absolute certainty*, without any reference to the ground of it, is frequently all that is meant by moral necessity. Thus, they build upon one idea of necessity, while they attack and defend themselves upon another idea thereof.

This is our present starting point then, agreed upon by all sides, that the foreknowledge of God infers the certainty of all future realities. Now, how can we conclude from hence, that the volitions of moral agents are, not only certain, but rendered certain by the influence of moral causes? It may be said, that it is sufficient that the foreknowledge of God proves that human volitions will certainly come to pass in some way or other; for if they will certainly come to pass in any way, we know that they must have some cause of their existence; and it is just as absurd to suppose that a volition can come into being without any cause of its existence, as it is to suppose that a world can come into being of itself. If this ground should be taken, (and it certainly will be,) the reply is obvious. It would show that the divine prescience can only prove the certainty of future events while it is left to the old maxim, that every effect must have a cause, in order to make out the doctrine of moral necessity, or the point in dispute! It would show, that after all the parade made with the divine prescience, it leaves the whole argument to rest upon ground which has already been occupied by one side, and fully considered by the other! It would only show, that a great pretence of demonstration had been made from the foreknowledge of God; whereas, in fact, it proves nothing to the purpose, unless "its most impotent and lame conclusion" be helped out by something else!

Another attempt is made to link the conclusion drawn from the foreknowledge of God, with the point to be established by the necessitarian. It is said, that God could not foreknow all future events, unless he views them as connected with known causes. This ground is taken by many eminent necessitarians. Thus, says Dr. John Dick, "Future events cannot be foreseen, unless they are certain; they cannot be certain, unless God have determined to bring them to pass."

The same position is assumed by President Edwards, "There must be a certainty in things themselves," says he, "before they are certainly foreknown." ... "There must be a certainty in things to be a ground of certainty of knowledge, and render things capable of being known to be certain." p. 122. Now, what is this certainty in things themselves, or in human volitions, without which they are incapable of being foreknown? The answer is obvious; for Edwards every where contends, that unless volitions are brought to pass by the *influence* of moral causes—that unless they are necessarily produced by an "effectual power and efficacy"—they are altogether uncertain and contingent, and connected with nothing that can render them certain. Hence, he clearly maintains, that unless human volitions are necessarily brought to pass by the influence of motives, they are not certain in themselves, and hence are incapable of being foreknown. And besides, he has a laboured argument to prove, that God could not foreknow the future volitions of moral agents, unless he views them as "necessarily connected with something else that is evident." pp. 115-117. This something else is not foreknowledge itself; for it is the ground of foreknowledge, it is the necessary influence of motives, or moral causes. But we need not dwell upon this point, as this is so evidently his meaning; and if it is not, then it is nothing to the purpose.

If Edwards means that a thing cannot be foreknown unless it has a sufficient ground and reason for its existence, and does not of itself come forth out of nothing, we are not at all concerned to deny his position. Every advocate of free-agency contends, that volition proceeds from the mind, acting in view of motives; and therefore is not destitute of a sufficient ground and reason of its existence. He denies that volition is necessarily brought to pass by the operation of motives. Hence, if Edwards merely means that God could not foreknow a human volition, unless he foreknew all the circumstances in view of the mind when it is to act, as well as the nature and all the circumstances of the mind from which the act is to proceed; no advocate of free-agency is at all concerned to deny his position. It may be true, or it may be false; but it establishes nothing which may not be consistently admitted by the advocates of free-agency. If he means any thing to the purpose, he must mean, that God could not foresee human volitions, unless they are necessarily connected with causes, according to his scheme of moral necessity; that is, unless they are necessarily produced by "the action or influence" of motives, or moral causes. If this is his meaning, then indeed it is something to the purpose; but what unbounded presumption is it, on the part of a poor blind worm of the dust, thus to set bounds and limits to the modes of knowledge possesssd by an infinite, all-knowing God! It is true, that "no understanding, created or uncreated, can see evidence where there is none"; but what kind of evidence that is, by which all things are rendered perfectly clear to the eye of Omniscience, it is surely not for us to determine. That all things are known to God, is freely admitted; but that they can be known, only by reason of their resulting from the necessitating influence of known causes, which are themselves necessitated, is more than any finite mind should presume to affirm. It were, indeed, to make our shallow, limited, and feeble intellects, the measure of all possible modes of knowledge. It were to make God like one of ourselves. Yet this position the necessitarian has been compelled to assume. After all his pretended demonstrations from the foreknowledge of God, his argument can reach the point in dispute, only by means of this tremendous flight of presumption.

Let the necessitarian show, that God cannot foresee future events, unless he "have determined to bring them to pass," or unless they are brought to pass by a chain of producing causes, ultimately connected with his own will; and he will prove something to the purpose. But let him not talk so boastfully about demonstrations, while there is this exceedingly weak link in the chain of his argument. If God were so like one of ourselves, that he could not foresee future volitions, unless they are brought to pass by the operation of known causes; then, I admit, that his foreknowledge would infer the moral necessity for which Edwards contends, provided he really possesses that knowledge; but if he were so imperfect a being, I should be compelled to believe, that there are some things which he could not foreknow.

This assumption comes with a peculiarly ill grace from the necessitarian. He should be the last man to contend, that God cannot foresee future events unless they are involved in known producing causes; just as all that we know of the future is ascertained by reasoning from known causes to effects. For he contends that with God, "there is no time"; but that to His view all things are seen as if they were present. His knowledge is without succession, and there is no before nor after with him; all things are intimately present to his mind from all eternity. Such is the doctrine of both the Edwardses; and Dr. Dick believes, that "God sees all things at a glance."

Now, present things are not known to exist, because they are implied by known causes, but because they are present and seen. And hence, if God sees all things as present, there is not the shadow of a foundation whereon to rest the proof of "moral necessity" from his foreknowledge. It is all taken away by their own doctrine, and their argument is left without the least support from it.

Indeed, there is no need of lugging the foreknowledge of God into the present controversy, except it be to deceive the mind. For all future events will certainly and infallibly come to pass, whether they are foreknown or not; and foreknowledge cannot make the matter any more certain than it is without it. We may say that God foreknows all things, and we may mix this up with all possible propositions; but this will never help the conclusion, that "all future things will certainly and infallibly come to pass." If God should cease to foreknow all future volitions, or if he had never foreknown them, they would, nevertheless, just as certainly and infallibly come to pass, as if he had foreknown them from all eternity. The bare naked fact, that they are future infers all that is implied in God's foreknowledge of them; and it is just as much a contradiction in terms, to say that what is future will not come to pass, as it is to say, that what God foreknows will never take place. Hence, by bringing in the prescience of Deity, we do not really strengthen or add to the conclusion in favour of necessity. It only furnishes a very convenient and plausible method of begging the question, or of seeming to prove something by hiding our sophisms in the blaze of the divine attributes. It only serves as a veil, behind which is concealed those sophistical tricks, by which both the performer and the spectator are deceived. This whole argument from the foreknowledge of God, is, indeed, a grand specimen of undesigned metaphysical jugglery, by which the mind is called off in one direction, whilst it is deceived, perplexed, and confounded, by not seeing what takes place in another.

It appears from these things, that those persons who have endeavoured to clear up this matter, by supposing that some things are not foreknown to God; have only got rid of one of the divine attributes, and not of their difficulty. It appears also, that Edwards might have made his argument far more simple and direct, by leaving out the long section in which he proves that God really foreknows all *future* things; and confining himself to the simple proposition, "that all future events will certainly and infallibly come to pass;" that "it is a contradiction in terms to say that a thing is future and yet that it will not come to pass"; or, in other words, "if a thing is future, *it is impossible it should be otherwise than true*," that it will come to pass. And how unreasonable are those, who have imagined that we are free-agents, because God has chosen not to foresee our free actions; as if the supposition that he might have foreseen them, does not infer necessity just as much as the fact that he does foresee them. Indeed, these reasoners seem to have expected to see one truth, by shutting their eyes upon another!

Mr. Hobbes has an argument to prove necessity, precisely like that of Edwards, except that its nakedness is not covered up with the foreknowledge of God. "Let the case be put," says he, "of the weather: 'tis necessary that tomorrow it shall rain or not rain. If, therefore, it be not necessary that it shall rain, it is necessary it shall not rain; otherwise there is no necessity that the proposition, it shall rain or not rain, should be true." This sophism confounds the *axiomatical necessity* referred to in the premise, that it must rain or not rain, with the *causal necessity* intended to be deduced from it in the conclusion. This poor sophism has been adopted by Mr. Locke, and seriously employed to prove that human volitions "cannot be free." Thus, says he, "It is unavoidably necessary to prefer the doing or forbearance of an action in a man's power, which is once proposed to a man's thoughts. The act of volition or preferring one of the two, being that, which he cannot avoid, a man in respect of that act of willing is under necessity." Here we have precisely the same confusion of an *axiomatical* with a *causal* necessity, that occurs in the argument of Mr. Hobbes. And yet, the younger Edwards has deemed this argument of Mr. Locke as worthy of his special notice and commendation; and President Day falls in with the same idea, alleging that "we will because we cannot avoid willing," because we must either choose or refuse. Is it not wonderful, that these philosophers should have imagined, that they had any controversy with any one, in contending so manfully that the mind, under certain circumstances, must either choose or refuse? or that they could infer any thing from this, in favour of a causal necessity—the only question in dispute? With what clearness! with what force! would President Edwards have dashed this poor flimsy sophism into a thousand atoms, if he had come across it in the atheism of Hobbes! But, unfortunately, he came across it in a different direction; and hence, he has rescued it from the loathsome dunghill of atheistical trash, invested it with dignity, seeming to clothe it in the solemn sanction of religion, by covering it up in the ample folds of the divine Omniscience.

This, then, is the conclusion of the whole matter. The prescience of God does not *make* our volitions necessary; it only *proves* them to be certain. This is conceded by Edwards. It proves them to be certain, just as present knowledge proves them to be certain. This also is admitted by Edwards. But present knowledge proves an act of the mind to be certain, because it is infallibly connected with that knowledge, and not because it is necessitated by the influence of a cause. It proves it to be certain, because it is impossible for a volition, or any thing else, not to exist at the time of its existence, and not because it is impossible for it to come to pass without being necessitated. In short, it proves an *axiomatical* and a *logical* necessity, but not a *causal* necessity; that is to say, it proves nothing to the point in dispute.

The necessitarian can connect his conclusion with the thing he has undertaken to prove, in only one of two ways: he may say, that if an event is certain, it cannot come into existence without a producing cause; or he may allege, that God cannot foresee them, unless he is determined to bring them to pass. If he takes the former position, he really discards the argument from foreknowledge, and returns for support to the old argument, that every effect must have a cause. And if he assumes the latter, maintaining that God cannot foreknow future events unless he reasons from producing causes to effects, he builds his argument, not upon foreknowledge alone, but upon this in connection with a most unwarrantable flight of presumption, without which the argument from prescience is good for nothing.

And besides, the bringing in of the divine prescience, only serves to blind, and not to illuminate. For God foreknows only what is future; and all future things will come to pass just as infallibly, without being foreknown, as they will with it. If we assume them to be future, it is just as much a contradiction to deny that they will come to pass; as it is to assume that they are foreknown and yet deny it. Nothing can be proved in this way, except what is assumed or taken for granted; and the foreknowledge of God is only a plausible way of begging the question, or concealing a sophism.

In conclusion, the necessitarian takes the wrong course in his inquiries, and lays his premises in the dark. To illustrate this point:—I know that I act; and hence, I conclude that God foreknew that I would act. And again, I know that my act is not necessitated, that it does necessarily proceed from the action, or influence of causes; and hence, I conclude that God foreknew that I would thus act freely, in precisely this manner, and not otherwise. Thus, I reason from what I know to what I do not know, from my knowledge of the actual world as it is, up to God's foreknowledge respecting it.

The necessitarian pursues the opposite course. He reasons from what he does not know, that is, from the particulars of the divine foreknowledge, about which he absolutely knows nothing *a priori*, down to the facts of the actual world. Thus, quitting the light which shines so brightly within us and around us, he seeks for light in the midst of impenetrable darkness. He endeavours to determine the phenomena of the world, not by looking at them and seeing what they are; but by deducing conclusions from God's infinite foreknowledge respecting them!

In doing this, a grand illusion is practised, by his merely supposing that the volitions themselves are foreknown, without taking into the supposition the whole of the case, and recollecting that God not only foresees all our actions, but also all about them. For if this were done, if it were remembered that He not only foresees that our volitions will come to pass, but also *how* they will come to pass; the necessitarian would see, that nothing could be proved in this way except what is first tacitly assumed. The grand illusion would vanish, and it would be clearly seen, that if the argument from foreknowledge proves any thing, it just as well proves the *necessity of freedom* as any thing else.

Indeed, it does seem to me, that it is one of the most wonderful phenomena in the history of the human mind, that, in reasoning about facts in relation to which the most direct and palpable sources of evidence are open before us, so many of its brightest ornaments should so long have endeavoured to draw conclusions from "the dark unknown" of God's foreknowledge; without perceiving that this is to reject the true method, to invert the true order of inquiry, and to involve the inquirer in all the darkness and confusion inseparable therefrom: without perceiving that no powers, however great, that no genius, however exalted, can possibly extort from such a method any thing but the dark, and confused, and perplexing exhibitions of an ingenious logomachy.

SECTION XII.

OF EDWARDS' USE OF THE TERM NECESSITY.

In the controversy concerning the will, nothing is of more importance, it will readily be admitted, than to guard against the influence of the ambiguity of words. Yet, it may be shown, that President Edwards has used the principal terms in this controversy in an exceedingly loose and indeterminate manner. This he has done especially in regard to the term *necessity*. His very definition prepares the way for such an abuse of language.

"*Philosophical necessity*," says he, "is really nothing else than the FULL AND FIXED CONNEXION BETWEEN THE THINGS SIGNIFIED BY THE SUBJECT AND PREDICATE OF A PROPOSITION, which affirms something to be true. When there is such a connexion, then the thing affirmed in the proposition is necessary, in a philosophical sense, whether any opposition or contrary effort be supposed or no. When the subject and predicate of the proposition, which affirms the existence of any thing, either substance, quality, act, or circumstance, have a full and CERTAIN CONNEXION, then the existence or being of that thing is said to be *necessary* in a metaphysical sense. And in this sense I use the word *Necessity*, in the following discourse, when I endeavour to prove *that Necessity is not inconsistent with Liberty*."

"The subject and predicate of a proposition, which affirms existence of something, may have a full, fixed, and certain connexion several ways."

"1. They may have a full and perfect connexion *in and of themselves;* because it may imply a contradiction, or gross absurdity, to suppose them not connected. Thus many things are necessary in their own nature. So the eternal existence of being, generally considered, is necessary *in itself;* because it would be in itself the greatest absurdity, to deny the existence of being in general, or to say there was absolute and universal nothing; and as it were the sum of all contradictions; as might be shown, if this were the proper place for it. So God's infinity, and other attributes are necessary. So it is necessary *in its own nature*, that two and two should be four; and it is necessary, that all right lines drawn from the centre to the circumference should be equal. It is necessary, fit, and suitable, that men should do to others, as they would that they should do to them. So innumerable metaphysical and mathematical truths are necessary *in themselves*; the subject and predicate of the proposition which affirms them, are perfectly connected of *themselves*."

"2. The connexion of the subject and predicate of a proposition, which affirms the existence of something, may be fixed and made certain, because the existence of that thing is *already* come to pass; and either now is, or has

94

been; and so has, as it were, made sure of existence. And therefore, the proposition which affirms present or past existence of it, may by this means, be made certain, and necessarily and unalterably true; the past event has fixed and decided the matter, as to its existence; and has made it impossible but that existence should be truly predicated of it. Thus the existence of whatever is already come to pass, is now become necessary; it is become impossible it should be otherwise than true, that such a thing has been."

"3. The subject and predicate of a proposition which affirms something to be, may have a real and certain connexion *consequentially*; and so the existence of the thing may be consequentially necessary, as it may be surely and firmly connected with something else, that is necessary in one of the former respects. As it is either fully and thoroughly connected with that which is absolutely necessary in its own nature; or with something which has already made sure of its existence. This necessity lies *in*, and may be explained *by*, the connexion between two or more propositions, one with another. Things which are *perfectly connected* with other things that are necessary, are necessary themselves, by a necessity of consequence."

After having defined what he means by philosophical or metaphysical necessity, he tells us, that this is the sense in which he uses the word, when he endeavours to show that necessity is not inconsistent with liberty. And yet under "this sense," how many totally distinct ideas are embraced! The eternal existence of being in general; the attributes of God; the proposition that two and two are four; the equality of the radii of a circle; the moral duty that we should do as we would be done by; the existence of a thing which has already come to pass; the existence of things, that are connected with that which is absolutely necessary in itself, or with something that has already made sure of its existence; the connexion of two or more propositions with each other—all these things are included in his definition of philosophical necessity! And yet he tells us, that he uses the term in this sense (in what sense?) when he undertakes to reconcile liberty with necessity! When he says, that he employs the word in *this* sense, one would suppose that, as a great metaphysician, he referred to some one of its precise and definite significations; but no such thing. He merely refers to its philosophical sense, which, according to his own explanation, embraces a multitude of different ideas. Hence, although he may keep close to this philosophical sense of the word, "in the ensuing discourse;" yet he may, before the discourse is concluded, shift his position a thousand times from one of these ideas to another. And he may always seem, to superficial observers, to speak of the same thing; because although the things spoken of are really different, they are all drawn together under one definition, and called by one name. He not only may have done this; he actually has done it. And if he had formed the express design to envelope the whole subject in a cloud of sophistry, he could not have taken a better course to accomplish his object.

It was the design of the Inquiry to establish the doctrine of moral necessity; and hence it was incumbent on President Edwards to reconcile this kind of necessity, and not philosophical necessity, with the free-agency of man. He contends that there is a necessary connexion between the influence of motives and volitions. This he calls moral necessity. It differs from natural necessity, says he, it differs from the necessary connexion between cause and effect; but yet, he expressly tells us, that this difference "does not lie so much *in the nature of the connexion*, as in the *terms connected*." In both cases, he maintains, the connexion is necessary and absolute. The two terms connected are different; but the kind and nature of the connexion is the same. This is the kind of necessity for which he pleads; and we can never be satisfied with his scheme, until the term shall be used in this precise and definite sense, and the doctrine it expresses shall be shown to be consistent with the true idea and feeling of liberty in the human breast. It will not, it cannot satisfy the mind, that any other kind of necessity is reconcilable with liberty; while it remains to be shown that moral necessity, as it is defined and explained in the Inquiry, is consistent with the free-agency of man.

There is one sense of the term in question, says he, "which especially belongs to the controversy about acts of the will," p. 30. It is what he calls "a necessity of consequence." This would be very true, if he merely meant by a necessity of consequence, to refer to the necessary connexion between cause and effect. But this is not his meaning; for he expressly says, that "a necessity of consequence" "lies *in*, and may be explained *by*, the connexion of two or more propositions one with another." Now what has the connexion between any two or all the propositions in the universe, to do with the controversy about acts of the will? Is it not evident, that it is the connexion which subsists between effects and their producing causes, and which is supposed to subsist between motives and actions, that has to do with the controversy in question; and that the connexion which subsists between two or more propositions is entirely foreign to the subject?

It may be said, that by "a necessity of consequence," Edwards referred not only to the connexion between two or more propositions, but also to the connexion between cause and effect. This is undoubtedly true; for he speaks of effects as coming to pass by this kind of necessity. But then it is to be lamented that two ideas, which are so perfectly distinct, should have been couched under the same mode of expression, and treated as if they were identically the same. Such a confounding of different ideas, has led to no little confusion and error in the reasoning of President Edwards.

The subject of the last section furnishes a striking illustration of the justness of this remark. From the proposition that a volition is certainly and infallibly foreknown, it follows, by a necessity of consequence, that it will come to pass. This is an instance of the necessary connexion between two ideas or propositions; between the idea or proposition, that a certain volition is foreknown, and the idea that it will come to pass; between the proposition which affirms that, it is foreknown, and the idea that it will come to pass in other words, the proposition which affirms that it is foreknown, necessarily assumes that it will come to pass; and to deny this assumption, at the same time that we make it, is surely to be guilty of a contradiction in terms. To suppose that a volition will not come to pass, is inconsistent with the proposition that it is certainly and infallibly foreknown. Edwards himself has frequently declared that this is the kind of necessity which is inferred from foreknowledge.

In truth, the necessary connexion which exists between the idea that a thing is foreknown, and the truth of the proposition which predicates future existence of it, is perfectly distinct from the necessary connexion between cause and effect. They are as widely different, as the connexion between any two propositions in Euclid is from the connexion between the motion of a ball and the force by which it is put in motion. Hence, the kind of necessity which is involved in the idea of foreknowledge, has nothing to do with the controversy about acts of the will.

There is, in like manner, a necessary connexion between the idea that a volition is now certainly and infallibly known to exist, and the truth of the proposition which affirms present existence of it; and hence, its present existence is necessary, by "a necessity of consequence," according to the definition of President Edwards. But all this has no relevancy to the question, as to *how* that volition came to pass. Its present existence is necessarily connected with the idea that it is certainly known to exist; but this is "a necessity of consequence" which "lies in, and may be explained by, the connexion between two or more propositions." It is not "a necessity of consequence" that lies *in*, or can be explained *by*, the connexion between cause and effect. The two things are entirely different, and it is strange, that they should always have been confounded by President Edwards. I do most certainly and infallibly know, for example, that I am now *willing* to write; and from this knowledge, it necessarily follows, that I am now *willing* to write.

But if any one should infer from hence, that I am necessitated to write, by the operation of some cause, we should certainly think his inference very badly drawn. Yet this is precisely the way in which the necessitarian proceeds, when he infers the necessity of human actions from the foreknowledge of God. He confounds the necessary connexion between two propositions, with the necessary connexion between cause and effect. This single ambiguity has been a mighty instrument in the building up of that portentous scheme of necessity, which has seemed to overshadow the glory and beauty of man's nature as a free and accountable being.

This is not the only ambiguity of the term in question which has been turned to account by the necessitarian. In opposition to the scheme of moral necessity, or the necessary connexion between volitions and the influence of motives, it has been said, that volitions are produced neither by motives, nor by preceding acts of choice. This is a direct denial of the doctrine of moral necessity, of the only thing which we are at all concerned to deny. We may thus attempt to escape from the thing, but the name still pursues us.

For, to this view of the subject, President Edwards replies as follows: "If any shall see cause to deny this, and say they hold no such thing as that every action is chosen or determined by a foregoing choice; but that the very first exertion of will only, undetermined by any preceding act, is properly called action; then I say, such a man's notion of action implies necessity; for what the mind is the subject of, without the determination of its own previous choice, it is the subject of necessarily, as to any hand that free choice has in the affair; and without any ability the mind has to prevent it, by any will or election of its own; because by the supposition it precludes all previous acts of the will or choice in the case, which might prevent it. So that it is again, in this other way, implied in the notion of an act, that, it is both necessary and not necessary," p. 199. It is in this manner, that President Edwards disposes of this important view of the subject of free-agency. Let us examine his logic.

In the first place, the argument is not sound. It proceeds on the supposition, that unless a volition is produced, it cannot be prevented, by a preceding act of volition. This is a false supposition. I choose, for example, to go out at one of the doors of my room. This choice is not produced by any preceding act of choice. And yet I can certainly prevent it, by choosing to go out at the other door of the room, or by choosing to sit still. Thus one act of choice may, from the very nature of things, necessarily exclude or prevent another act of choice; although it could not possibly have produced that other act of choice.

But suppose the argument to be sound, what does it prove? It proves our actions to be necessary; but in what sense? Does it show them to be subject to that moral necessity, for which Edwards contends, and against which we protest? This is the question, let me repeat, which we have undertaken to discuss; and if we would not wander in an eternal maze of words, we must keep to it; it is the talisman which is to conduct us out of all our difficulties and perplexities. It is the first point, and the second point, and the third point in logic, to keep to the issue, steadily, constantly, and without the least shadow of turning. Otherwise we shall lose ourselves in a labyrinth of words, in darkness and confusion interminable.

In what sense, then, does the above argument, supposing it to be sound, prove our actions to be necessary? Does it prove them to be necessary with a moral necessity? It does not. According to the argument in question, volitions are necessary, "*as to any hand free choice has in the affair; because by the supposition* it precludes all previous acts of the will or choice in the case, *which might prevent them.*" That is to say, volitions are necessary as to previous acts of choice; because *by the supposition* previous acts of choice do not produce them, and consequently cannot prevent them. This is the argument.

Now, it is very true, that this is not an unheard of use of the term in question. We say a thing is necessary, when it is dependent upon no cause for its existence. Thus the existence of the Supreme Being is said to be necessary, because he is the uncaused Cause of all things. As he owes his existence to nothing, so there is nothing capable of destroying it. He is independent of all causes; and hence, his existence is said to be necessary.

In like manner, a thing may be said to be necessary as to any other particular thing, upon which it does not depend for its existence. As the Supreme Being is said to be necessary as to all things, because his existence depends upon nothing; so any created object may be said to be necessary, as to the influence of any other object, to which it does not owe its existence, and upon which its existence does not depend. It is in this sense that our volitions are shown to be necessary by the above argument of President Edwards. A volition "is necessary as to any hand free choice has in the affair; because by the supposition it preclude all previous acts of the will or choice in the case, which might prevent it." That is to say, it is necessary as to preceding acts of choice; because, by the supposition, it is wholly independent of preceding acts of choice for its existence.

Now, in so far as the doctrine of moral necessity is concerned, this argument amounts to just exactly nothing. For although a volition may be necessary as to one particular cause, in consequence of its being wholly independent of that cause; it does not follow that it is necessarily produced by another cause. Because it does not result from any preceding act of volition, and consequently is necessary as to any hand that preceding act of volition had in the affair, it does not follow, that the "strongest motive" produces it. Supposing a volition to be independent of all causes, as well as of preceding acts of choice; and then it would be necessary, in the same sense, as to all causes, as well as to preceding acts of choice. But how infinitely absurd would it be to conclude, that because a volition is independent of the influence of all causes, it is therefore necessarily connected with the influence of a particular cause!

We only deny that volitions are necessarily connected with the "power," or "influence," or "action," of motives or moral causes. This is the only kind of necessity against which, as the advocates of free-agency, we are at all concerned to contend. And it is worse than idle for the necessitarian to endeavour to establish any other kind of necessity beside this. Let him come directly to the point, and *keep to it*, if he would hope to accomplish any thing. This shifting backwards and forwards from one meaning of an ambiguous term to another; this showing a volition to be necessary in one sense, and then tacitly assuming it to be necessary in another sense; is not the way to silence and refute the adversaries of the doctrine of moral necessity. It may show, (supposing the argument to be sound,) that a volition is necessary as to a particular cause, on the supposition that it is not produced by that cause; and in the same manner, it might be shown, that a volition is necessary as to all causes, on the supposition that it is produced by no cause. But the necessity which results from such a supposition, would be directly arrayed against the necessity for which President Edwards contends. In the same sense, volitions "are necessary as to any hand motives have in the affair," on the supposition that they do not result from the influence of motives; but instead of building on this kind of necessity, one would have supposed that President Edwards was somewhat concerned in its destruction.

In short, the case stands thus: a thing is said to be necessary, on the supposition that it has *no cause* of its existence; or necessary as to another thing, on the supposition that it does not depend on that other thing for its existence. Again, a thing is said to be necessary, on the supposition that it proceeds from the operation of *a cause*. These ideas are perfectly distinct. The difference between them is as clear as noonday. It is true, they have the same name; but to reason from the one to the other, is about as wild an abuse of language as could be made. President Edwards is required to show that a volition is necessary, in the sense of *its having a moral cause;* he has shown that it is necessary in the sense of *its not having a cause.* This is his argument.

Let us view this subject in another light. If we say that a volition proceeds from a prior act of choice, we certainly hold the doctrine of necessity. President Edwards speaks out from the Inquiry and convicts us of this doctrine. "Their notion of, action," says he, "implies necessity, and supposes that it is necessary, and cannot be contingent. For they suppose, that whatever is properly called action, must be determined by the will and free choice; and this is as much as to say, that it must be necessary, being dependent upon, and determined by something foregoing; namely, a foregoing act of choice," p. 199. Thus, if we say that a volition is produced by a preceding act of volition, we are clearly convicted of the doctrine of necessity.

Now let us endeavour to escape from this accusation. For this purpose, let us assume the directly opposite position: let us deny that our volitions are produced by preceding acts of choice—and what then? Are we out of danger? Far from it. We are still convicted of the dreaded doctrine of necessity. On the very supposition we have made, diametrically opposite as it is to the former, we are still convicted of the same doctrine of necessity. We cannot escape from it. It pursues us, like a ghost, through the dark and ill-defined shadows of an ambiguous phraseology, and lays its cold hand upon us. Turn wheresoever we may, it is sure to meet us in some shape or other.

This is not all. We are also convicted of a contradiction in terms. It is shown, that we hold an act to be "both necessary and not necessary." This may appear to be an exceedingly grave charge; and yet I think we may venture to put in the plea of "guilty." We do hold an act to be necessary, as to the strongest motive, as well as to any preceding act of choice, by which we contend it is not produced, and by which it cannot be prevented. We likewise most freely admit, that many volitions are necessary in other senses of the word, as explained by President Edwards. We cannot deny this, so long as we retain our senses; for "a thing is said to be necessary," according to him, "when it has already come to pass, and so made sure of its existence; and it is likewise said to be necessary, when its present existence, is certainly and infallibly known, as well as when its future existence is certainly and infallibly foreknown. But yet we deny, that an act of volition is necessary, in the sense that it is produced by the operation of the strongest motive, as it is called. That is to say, we admit an act of choice to be necessary, in some senses of the word; and, in another sense of it, we deny it to be necessary." Is there any thing very contradictory in all this? Any thing to shock the common sense and reason of mankind?

It may be said, that Edwards does not always endeavour to establish the doctrine of moral necessity; that he frequently aims merely to show, that our actions are "not without all necessity." This is unquestionably true. He frequently arrives at this conclusion; and he seems to think that he has done something, whenever he has shown our actions to be necessary in any sense of the word as defined by himself. But it is difficult to conceive with whom he could have had any controversy. For certainly no one in his right mind, could pretend to deny that human actions are necessary in any sense, as the word is explained and used in the Inquiry. When it is said, for example, that the truth of the proposition which affirms the future existence of an event, is *necessarily* connected with the idea that that event is certainly and infallibly foreknown; no one, in his right mind, can deny the position. Such a denial, as Edwards says, involves a contradiction in terms. Hence, this notion of necessity only requires to be stated and understood, in order to rivet irresistible conviction on the mind of every rational being. No light has been thrown upon it, by the pages which President Edwards has devoted to the subject; nor could a thousand volumes render it one whit clearer than it is in itself. Hence, the author of the Inquiry should have seen, that if there was any controversy with him on this point, it was not because there was any diversity of opinion; but because there was a misconception of his proposition. And no doubt he would have seen this, if the meaning of his own language had been clearly defined in his own mind: if he had marked out and circumscribed, as with a sunbeam, the precise limitation within which his own propositions are true, and beyond which they are false.

If he had done this, he would have seen that there was, and that there could have been, but one real point of difference between himself and his adversaries. He would have seen, that, aside from the ambiguities of language, there was but one real point in dispute. He would have seen, that it was affirmed, on the one side, that the strongest motive operates to produce a choice; and that this was denied on the other. And hence, he would have put forth his whole strength to establish this single point, to fortify this single doctrine of moral necessity. He would not have crowded so many different ideas into the definition of the term *necessity*; and then imagined that he was overwhelming and confounding his adversaries, when he was only showing that human "actions are not without all necessity." And when they said, that "a necessary action is a contradiction," he would have seen how they used the term necessary; and he would not have concluded, as he has done, that this "notion of action implies contingence, *and excludes all necessity*," p. 199. He

102

would have seen, that the idea of an action, in our view, is inconsistent with necessity, in one sense of the word; and yet not inconsistent with every thing that has been called necessity.

In the definition of President Edwards, there is an inherent and radical defect, which I have not as yet noticed; and which is, indeed, the source of all his vacillating on this subject. It proceeds from a very common error, which has been well explained and illustrated by Mr. Stewart in his Essay on the Beautiful.

The various theories, which ingenious men have framed in relation to the beautiful, says Mr. Stewart, "have originated in a prejudice, which has descended to modern times from the scholastic ages; that when a word admits of a variety of significations, these different significations must all be *species* of the same *genus*; and must consequently include some essential idea common to every individual to which the generic term can be applied."

The question of Aristippas, "how can beauty differ from beauty," says Mr. Stewart, "plainly proceeded on a total misconception of the nature of the circumstances; which, in the history of language, attach different meanings to the same word; and which by slow and insensible gradations, remove them to such a distance from their primitive or radical sense, that no ingenuity can trace the successive steps of their progress. The variety of these circumstances is, in fact, so great, that it is impossible to attempt a complete enumeration of them; and I shall, therefore, select a few of the cases, in which the principle now in question appears most obviously and indisputably to fail."

"I shall begin with supposing, that the letters A, B, C, D, E, denote a series of objects; that A possesses some quality in common with B; B a quality in common with C; C a quality in common with D; D a quality in common with E;—while at the same time, no quality can be found which belongs in common to any *three* objects in the series. Is it not conceivable, that the affinity between A and B may produce a transference of the name of the first to the second; and that, in consequence of the other affinities which connect the remaining objects together, the same name may pass in succession from B to C; from C to D; and from D to E?"

This idea, and the reasoning which Mr. Stewart has founded upon it, are at once obvious, original and profound. It shows that the most gifted philosophers, have not been able to frame a satisfactory theory of the beautiful, because they have proceeded on the false supposition, that all those objects which are called beautiful have some common property, merely because they have a common appellation, by which they are distinguished from other objects; and that in endeavouring to point out and define this common property, they have engaged in an impracticable attempt; and hence they have succeeded to their own satisfaction, only by doing violence to the nature of things.

This is a fruitful idea. It admits of many illustrations. I shall select only a few. Philosophers and jurists have frequently attempted to define executive power; but they have proceeded on the supposition, that all those powers called executive, have a common and distinguishing property, because they have a common name. Hence, they have necessarily failed; because the supposition on which they have proceeded is false. Executive power, properly so called, is that which sees to the execution of the laws; and other powers are called executive, not because they partake of the nature of such powers, but simply because they have been conferred upon the chief executive magistrate.

The same remark, may be made, in relation to the attempts of ingenious men, to define the nature of law in general. If we analyze all those things which have been called laws, we shall find that they have no element or property in common: the only thing they have in common is the name. Hence, when we undertake to define law in general, or to point out the common property by which laws are distinguished from other things, we must necessarily fail. We may frame a definition in words, as others have done; but, however carefully this may be constructed, it can be applied to different kinds of laws, only by giving totally different meanings to the words of which it is composed. Thus, for example, a law is said to be "a rule of conduct," given by a superior to an inferior, and "which the inferior is bound to obey." Now, who does not see, that the words *conduct* and *obedience*, must have totally distinct meanings, when they are applied to inanimate objects and when they are applied to the actions of moral and accountable beings? And who does not see, that human beings are *bound* to do their duty, in an entirely different sense, from that in which matter can be said to be under an obligation? The same remark may be extended to all the definitions which have been given of law in general. And whoever understands the philosophy of definitions, will easily perceive that every attempt to draw things, so wholly unlike each other, under one and the same mode of expression, is not really to define, but to hide, the true nature of things under the ambiguities of language.

Of this common fault, President Edwards has been guilty. Instead of defining the various senses of the term necessity, and always using it with precision and without confusion; he has undertaken to show wherein those things called necessary really agree in some common property. He looked for a common nature, where there is only a common name. As Aristippas could not conceive, "how beauty could differ from beauty;" so, if we may judge from his argument, it was a great difficulty with him, to conceive how necessity can differ from necessity. Hence, when he proves an action to be necessary in any one of the various senses which are included under his definition of philosophical necessity, he imagines that his work is done; and when his adversary denies that an action is necessary in any one of those senses, he concludes that he denies "all necessity!" In all this, we see the question as plainly as if it had been expressly written down, "how can philosophical necessity differ from philosophical necessity?" To which I would simply reply, that a thing cannot differ from itself, it is true; but the same word may have very different meanings; and that it is "a prejudice which has descended to modern times from the scholastic ages," to suppose that things have a common nature, merely because they have a common name.

No better illustration of the fallacy of this prejudice could be furnished, than that which Edwards has given in his definition of philosophical or metaphysical necessity. Under this definition, as we have seen, he has included the being of a God, which is said to be necessary, because he has existed from all eternity, unmade and uncaused; and also the existence of an effect, which is said to be necessary, because it necessarily results from the operation of a cause. Now, these two ideas stand in direct opposition to each other; and the only thing they have in common is the name. And yet President Edwards reasons from the one to the other! If he can, in any way, reach the name, this seems to satisfy him. The *thing* in dispute is entirely overlooked. If we say that choice is produced by choice, then he contends it is an effect, and consequently necessary. If we deny that choice is produced by choice, then it is necessary any how; not because it is produced by a cause, but because it is independent of a cause, being neither produced nor prevented by it. It makes no difference with this great champion of necessity, whether choice is said to be produced by choice or not; for, on either of these opposite suppositions, he can show that our volitions are necessary. The absence of the very circumstance which makes it necessary in the one case, is that which makes it necessary in the other. Is choice produced by choice? Then this dependence of choice upon choice, shows it to be necessary. Is choice *not* produced by choice? Then this independence of choice upon choice is the very thing which shows it to be necessary! Thus this great champion of necessity, just passes from one meaning of the term to another, without the least regard to the point in dispute, or to the logical coherency of his argument. Surely, if "a reluctant world has bowed in homage" to his logic, it must have been because the world has been too indolent to pry into the sophisms with which it swarms. It is only in his onsets upon error, that the might of his resistless logic is felt; in the defence of his own system, he does not reason at all, he merely rambles. Indeed, with all his gigantic power, he was compelled to reel and stagger under the burden of such a cause.

SECTION XIII.

OF NATURAL AND MORAL NECESSITY.

I HAVE already said many things bearing upon the famous distinction between natural and moral necessity; but this distinction is regarded as so important by its advocates, that it deserves a separate notice. This I shall proceed to give it.

The distinction in question is treated with no great reverence by the advocates of free-agency. It is denounced by them as a distinction without a difference; and, though this may be true in the main, yet this is not the way to settle any thing. There is, indeed, a real difference between natural and moral necessity, as they are held and described by necessitarians; and if we pay no attention to it, our declarations about its futility will be apt to produce more heat than light. I fully recognize the justness of the demand made by Dr. Edwards, that those who insist that natural and moral necessity are the same, should tell us in what respects they are so. "We have informed them," says he, "in what respects we hold them to be different. We wish them to be equally explicit and candid," p. 19. I intend to be equally explicit and candid.

I admit, then, that there is a real difference between natural and moral necessity; they differ, as the Edwardses say, in the nature of the terms connected. In the one case, there is a natural cause and its effect, such as force and the motion produced by it, connected together; and in the other, there is a motive and a volition. In this respect, I believe that there is a greater difference between them than does the necessitarian himself; for he considers volition to be of the same nature with an effect, whereas I regard it as essentially different in nature and in kind from an effect.

There is another difference between natural and moral necessity. Natural necessity admits of an opposition of the will; whereas it is absurd to suppose any such opposition in the case of moral necessity. A man may be so bound that his utmost efforts to move may prove unavailing: in such a case, he is said to labour under a natural necessity. This always implies and presupposes an opposition of will. But not so in regard to moral necessity. It is absurd to suppose, that our wills can ever be in opposition to moral necessity; for this would be to suppose that we are made willing by the influence of motives, and yet are not willing.

Now, I fully recognize these differences between natural and moral necessity, as they are viewed by the necessitarian. Whether they are not inconsistent with their ideas of moral necessity, is another question. But as I am not concerned with that question at present, I am willing to take these differences without the least abatement. Admitting, then, that these distinctions are well-founded, and that they are perfectly consistent with the idea of moral necessity, let us see in what respects there is an agreement between the things under consideration. The difference does not lie, says Edwards, *so much in the nature of the connexion*, as in the two terms connected. Moral necessity is "a sure and perfect connexion between moral causes and effects." It is "as absolute as natural necessity." The influence of motives is not a condition of volition, which the will may or may not follow; it is the *cause* thereof; and it is absurd to suppose that the effect, the volition, can be loose from the influence of its cause, p. 77-8. Yes, volition is just as absolutely and unconditionally controlled by motive, as the inanimate objects of nature are controlled by the power of the Almighty. The connexion, the necessary connexion, which subsists between motion and the force by which it is produced, is the same in nature and in kind as that which subsists between the "action or influence of motive" and volition. Herein, then, is the agreement, that in moral necessity, as well as in natural, the effect is produced by the influence of its cause. The nature of the connexion is the same in both; and in both it is equally absolute.

Now we have seen the differences, and we have also seen the points of agreement; and the question is, not whether this famous distinction be well-founded, but whether it will serve the purpose for which it is employed. In the full light, and in the perfect recognition of this distinction, we deny that it will serve the purpose of the necessitarian.

It is supposed, that natural necessity alone interferes with the free-agency of man, while moral necessity is perfectly consistent with it. But, in reality, moral necessity is more utterly subversive of all free-agency and accountability than natural necessity itself. Think not that this is a mere hasty and idle assertion. Let us look at it, and see if it is not true.

We have already seen, that a caused volition is no volition at all;—that a necessary agent is a contradiction in terms. In other words, a power to act must itself act, and not be made to act by the action of any other power, or else it does not act at all. And if it must be caused to act, before it can act, then, as we have already seen, there must be an infinite series of acts. These things have been fully illustrated, and defended against the false analogies, by which they have been assailed; and they are here mentioned only for the sake of greater clearness and distinctness.

If the scheme of moral necessity be true, then, according to which our volitions are absolutely caused by the "action or influence of motive," it is idle to talk about free acts of the will; for there are no acts of the will at all. If our wills are caused to put forth volitions, and are turned to one side or the other, by the controlling influence of motives, it is idle to talk about a free-will; for we have no will at all. I know full well, that President Edwards admits that we have a will; and that the will does really act; but this admission is contradicted by bringing the will and all its exercises under the domination and absolute control of motives. He obliterates the distinction between cause and effect, between action and passion, between mental activity and bodily motion; and thereby draws the phenomena of will, the volitions of all intelligent creatures, under the iron scheme of necessity. We are eternally reminded that Edwards believes in the existence of a will, and in the reality of its acts. We know it; but let us not be accused of misrepresenting him, unless it can be shown that one part of his system does not contradict another,— unless it can be shown, not by false analogies and an abuse of words, but by valid evidence, that *an act of the mind may be necessarily caused*. This never has been shown; and the attempts of the necessitarian to show it, as we have seen, are among the most signal failures in the whole range of human philosophy. Until this be shown, we must contend that there is nothing in the universe so diametrically opposed to all free-agency—to all liberty of the will, as the scheme of moral necessity; which so clearly overthrows and, demolishes the very idea of a will and all its volitions.

Indeed, what is called natural necessity does not properly interfere with the liberty of *the will* at all; it merely restrains the freedom of *motion*. It is moral necessity that reaches the seat of the mind, and takes away all the freedom thereof; even denying to us the possession of a will itself. When my hand is bound, I may strive to move it in vain; in this case, my *will* is free, because I may strive, or I may not; but the hand is not free, because it cannot move. But if motives cause the mind to follow their influence, so that it may not possibly depart or be loose from that influence; then we have no will at all; and it is idle and a mockery to talk about freedom of the will. And yet, although Edwards would have us to believe that no system is consistent with free-agency but his own; he occupies the position, that it is absurd to suppose, that a volition may possibly be loose from the influence of motive; that this is to suppose that it is the effect of motive, and at the same time that it is not the effect of motive!

"All agree," says Day, "that a necessity which is opposed to our choice, is inconsistent with liberty," p. 91. That is to say, a necessity which cuts off or prevents the external consequence of our choice, is inconsistent with liberty of the will; but that which takes away one choice, and sets up another, is perfectly consistent with it! If the arm is held, so that the free choice cannot move it, then is the liberty of the will interfered with; but, though the will may be absolutely swayed and controlled, by the influence of motives, or by the sovereign power of God himself, yet is it perfectly free! If such be the liberty of the will, what is it worth?

There are many things, which it is beyond the power of the human mind to accomplish. Even in such cases, the natural necessity under which we are said to labour, does not interfere with the liberty of the will. If we cannot do such things, it is not because our will is not free in regard to them, but because its power is limited. We might very well attempt them, and put forth volitions in order to accomplish them, as in our ignorance we often do; and if we abstain from so doing in other cases, wherein we might wish to act, it is because we know they are beyond our power, and, as rational creatures, do not choose to make fools of ourselves. To say that we are under a natural necessity, then, is only to say that our power is limited, and not that it is not free. It is reserved for moral necessity—shall I say to enslave?—no, but to annihilate the will.

It is true, if we will to do a thing, and are restrained from doing it by a superior force, we are not to blame for not doing it; or if we refuse to do it, and are constrained to do it, we are equally blameless. In such cases, natural necessity, although it does not reach the will, is an excuse for external conduct. If the question were, is a man accountable for his external actions? for the movements of his body? then we might talk about natural necessity. But as the question, in the present controversy, is, whether a man is accountable for his internal acts, for the volitions of his mind? to talk about natural necessity is wholly irrelevant. It has nothing to do with such a controversy; and hence, Edwards is entirely mistaken when he supposes that it is natural necessity, and that alone, which is opposed to the freedom of the will. It is in fact opposed to nothing but the freedom of the body; and by lugging it into the present controversy, it can only serve to make confusion the worse confounded.

It is the general sentiment of mankind, that moral necessity is inconsistent with free-agency and accountability. Edwards has taken great pains to explain this fact. His great reason for it is, that men are in the habit of excusing themselves for their outward conduct, on the ground of natural necessity. In this way, by early and constant association, the idea of blamelessness becomes firmly attached to the term necessity, as well as those terms, such as must, cannot, &c., in which the same thing is implied. Hence, we naturally suppose that we are excusable for those things which are necessary with a moral necessity. Thus, the fact that men generally regard moral necessity and free-agency as incompatible with each other, is supposed by Edwards to arise from the ambiguity of language; and that if we will only shake off this influence, we shall see a perfect agreement and harmony between them.

But is this so? Let any man fix his mind upon the very idea of moral necessity itself, and then answer this question. Let him lay aside the term necessity, and all kindred words; let him simply and abstractedly consider a volition as being produced by the "action or influence of motives;" and then ask himself, if the subject in which this effect is produced is accountable for it? If it can be his virtue or his vice? Let him conceive of a volition, or anything else, as being produced in the human mind, by an extraneous cause; and then ask himself if the mind in which it is thus produced can be to praise or to blame for it? Let any man do this, and I think he will see a better reason for the common sentiment of mankind than any which Edwards has assigned for it; he will see that men have generally regarded moral necessity as incompatible with free-agency and accountability, just because it is utterly irreconcilable with them.

Indeed, however liable "the common people," and philosophers too, may be to be deceived and misled by the ambiguities of language, there is no such deception in the present case. The common people, as they are called, do not always say, my actions are "necessary," "I cannot help them," and therefore I am not accountable for them. They as frequently say, that if my actions, if my volitions, are brought to pass by the strength and influence of motives, I am not responsible for them. This common sentiment and conviction of mankind, therefore, does not blindly aim merely at the name, while it misses the thing; it does indeed bear with all its force directly upon the scheme of moral necessity itself. And its power is sought to be evaded, as we have seen, and as we shall still further see, not by explaining the ambiguities of language, so as to enlighten mankind, but by confounding the most opposite natures, such as action and passion, volition and local motion, through the ambiguities of language. It is the necessitarian, who is always talking about the ambiguities of language, that is continually building upon them. Indeed, it is hard to conceive why he has so often been supposed to use language with such wonderful precision, if it be not because he is eternally complaining of the want of it in others.

Just let the common people, or those of them who may desire an opiate for their consciences, see the scheme of moral necessity as it is in itself, stripped of all the disguises of an ambiguous phraseology, and it will satisfy them. It will be the one thing needful to their craving and hungering appetites. Let them be made to believe that all our volitions are produced by the action and influence of motives, so that they may not be otherwise than they are; and a sense of moral obligation and responsibility will be extinguished in their breasts, unless nature should prove too strong for sophistry. Indeed, if we may believe the most authentic accounts, this doctrine has done its strange and fearful work among the common people, both in this country and in Europe. It is a philosophy which is within the reach of the most ordinary minds, as well as the most agreeable to the most abandoned hearts; and hence its awfully desolating power. And if its ravages and devastations have not extended wider and deeper than they have, it is because they have been checked by the combined powers of nature and of religion, rather than by logic; by the happy inconsistency, rather than by the superior metaphysical acumen, of its advocates and admirers.

SECTION XIV.

OF EDWARDS' IDEA OF LIBERTY.

It was not the design of Edwards, as it is well known, to interfere with the moral agency of man. He honestly believed that the scheme of necessity, as held by himself, was perfectly consistent with the doctrine of liberty; and he retorted upon his adversaries that it was their system, and not his, which struck at the foundation of moral agency and accountability. But however upright may have been his intentions, he has merely left us the name of liberty, while he has in reality denied to us its nature and its essence.

According to his view of the subject, "The plain and obvious meaning of the words freedom and liberty, in common speech, is the *power, opportunity,* or *advantage that any one has to do as he pleases.* Or, in other words, his being free from hindrance or impediment in the way of doing, or conducting in any respect as he wills. And the contrary to liberty, whatever name we call that by, is a person's being hindered, or unable to conduct as he will, or being necessitated to do otherwise."

This is the kind of liberty for which he contends. And he says, "There are two things contrary to what is called liberty in common speech. One is *constraint,* otherwise called *force, compulsion,* and *co-action,* which is a person's being necessitated to do a thing *contrary* to his will. The other is *restraint*; which is his being hindered, and not having power to do *according* to his will. But that which has no will cannot be the subject of these things."

This notion of liberty, as Edwards says, presupposes the existence of a will. In fact, it presupposes more than this; it presupposes the existence of a determination of the will. For, unless one is determined not to do a thing, he cannot be constrained to do it, contrary to his will; and, unless he is determined to do a thing, he cannot be restrained from doing it according to his will. This kind of liberty, then, as it presupposes the existence of a determination of the will, has nothing to do with the manner in which that determination is brought to pass. If the determination of the mind or will were brought to pass, so to speak, by an absolutely irresistible force; just as any other effect is brought to pass by its efficient cause; yet this kind of liberty might exist in its utmost perfection. For it only requires that after the will is determined in this manner, or in any other, that it should be left free from *constraint* or *restraint,* to flow on just as it has been determined to do. It is no other liberty than that which is possessed by a current of water, when it is said to flow *freely,* because it is not opposed in its course by any material obstruction.

That the liberty for which Edwards contends, has nothing to do with the manner in which our actions or volitions come to pass; or, more properly speaking, with the kind of relation between motives and actions, we have his own express acknowledgment. "What is vulgarly called liberty," says he, "namely, that power and opportunity for one to do and conduct as he will, or according to his choice, is all that is meant by it; without taking into the meaning of the word *any thing of the cause of that choice; or at all considering how the person came to have such a volition;* whether it was caused by some *external motive,* or *internal habitual bias;* whether it was determined by some internal antecedent volition, or whether it happened without a cause; whether *it was necessarily connected with something foregoing, or not connected. Let the person come by his choice* ANY HOW, yet if he is able, and there is nothing in the way to hinder his pursuing and executing his will, *the man is perfectly free,* according to the primary and common notion of freedom."

This notion of liberty, it is easy to see, is consistent with the most absolute scheme of fatality of which it is possible to conceive. For, according to this idea of it, if we should come by our choice "any how," even by the most irresistible influence of external circumstances, yet we might be "perfectly free." Hence it is no wonder that we find the same definition of liberty in the writings of the most absolute fatalists.

It is remarkable that Edwards has taken great pains to define his idea of philosophical necessity, and to distinguish it from the common sense of the word; and yet he supposes that the notion of liberty, about which the same dispute is conversant, is that which is referred to "in common speech," or that "which is vulgarly called liberty." He contends for a *philosophical necessity,* and especially for a necessary connexion between the influence of motives and volitions; but the *philosophical liberty* which stands opposed to his scheme, which denies any such *necessary* connexion, he has not deemed it worth his while to notice!

Liberty, according to Edwards' sense of the term, has nothing to do with the controversy respecting free-agency and necessity. It is as consistent with fatalism as could be desired by the most extravagant supporters of that odious system. Hence, when the doctrine of necessity is denied, and that of liberty or moral agency is asserted, something more than this is intended. The idea of liberty, as it stands connected with the controversy in question, has reference to the manner in which our volitions come to pass, to the relation which subsists between motives and their corresponding actions. When we say that

114

the will is free, we mean "that it is not necessarily determined by the influence of motives;" we mean to deny the doctrine of moral necessity, or that the relation which subsists between a motive and its corresponding act, is not that which subsists between an efficient cause and its effect. We mean to contend for a philosophical liberty, as President Edwards contends for a philosophical necessity, and not for that "which is vulgarly called liberty."

There is an inconsistency, I am aware, in supposing a choice to be induced by the force of external circumstances, or by the force of motives, whether external or internal; but this inconsistency belongs to the scheme of necessity; and if I have indulged in the supposition for a moment, it was only to meet the necessitarian, and argue with him on his own ground. As I have already said, a will that is *determined*, instead of *determining*, is no will at all. And the liberty of the will for which we contend, is implied by the power of the mind to ACT. It does not depend upon the presence or the absence of any external obstruction. It is no such occasional, or accidental thing; it is an inherent and essential attribute and power of the mind. No power in the universe, but that of creation, can produce it, and no chains on earth can bind it.

The idea of liberty, as contended for by President Edwards, is no other than that entertained by Mr. Locke. Thus, says the latter, "there may be thought, there may be will, there may be *volition, where there is no liberty.*" In illustration of this position he says, "A man falling into water, (a bridge breaking under him,) has not herein liberty, is not a free-agent. For though he has *volition*, though he prefers his not falling to falling, yet the forbearance of that motion not being in his power, the stop or cessation of that motion follows not upon his volition; and therefore therein he is not free."

It is true, he is not therein free, in one of the most common senses of the term; but it is wrong to conclude from hence, that there is in such a case, "*no liberty.*" For if the volition, of which he is said to be possessed, did not result from the action of any thing, if it was simply an act of the mind, which was not necessarily produced by another act, then he possessed freedom in the philosophical sense of the term. He was free in the act of willing, in the possession of his volition, although the consequence of that volition was cut off and prevented by an over-ruling necessity, which had no conceivable relation to the manner in which he came by his volition. Wherever there is a volition, there is this kind of liberty; for a volition is not, and cannot be, produced by any coercive force.

The foregoing illustration might have been very consistently offered by President Edwards, who considered a volition and a preference of the mind as identically the same; but it comes not with so good a grace from Mr. Locke.

He considered an act of the will as different from a preference. According to his doctrine, a man might prefer not to fall, in such a case as that put by himself, and yet not will not to fall. And he illustrates the difference by saying, "a man would prefer flying to walking, yet who can say he ever wills it?" Now, if a man cannot will to fly, it is very difficult to see how he can will not to fall, in case he were dropped from the air.

The illustration of Mr. Locke is fallacious. It does not show, and I humbly conceive it cannot be shown, that there can be a volition anywhere in the universe where there is not freedom. The very idea of a volition, or an act of the mind, necessarily implies that kind of philosophical liberty for which we contend.

The above notion of liberty, which Mr. Locke borrowed from Hobbes, and Edwards from Locke, evidently confounds the motion of the body, (which they frequently call action,) with volition or action of the mind. Thus, no matter how a volition comes to pass, or is caused to exist, if there is nothing to prevent the *motion* of the body from following its influence, we are said to be perfectly free. This kind of liberty, therefore, refers to the motion of the body, and not to the action of the mind. It has no reference whatever to the question, Is the mind free in the act of willing? This is the question in dispute; and hence, if the necessitarian would say any thing to the purpose, he must show that his scheme is reconcilable with the freedom of the mind in willing. This Edwards has not attempted to do. He has, in fact, as we have seen, only given us the name, while he has taken from us the substance of liberty.

The idea of liberty, for which Edwards contends, may be illustrated by an unobstructed fall of water. Indeed, this is the very thing by which Mr. Hobbes has chosen to illustrate and explain it. "I conceive liberty to be rightly defined in this manner," says he; "liberty is the absence of all the impediments to action, (motion?) that are not contained in the nature and intrinsical quality of the agent, as for example, the water is said to descend freely, or to have liberty to descend by the channel of the river, because there is no impediment that way, but not across, because the banks are impediments, and though the water cannot ascend, yet men never say it wants the liberty to ascend, but the faculty or power, because the impediment is in the nature of the water, and intrinsical." Mr. Hobbes encountered no more difficulty in reconciling this notion of liberty with the scheme of fatality for which he contended, than President Edwards found in reconciling it with the same scheme in disguise.

According to the Inquiry, then, we have no other liberty than that which may be ascribed to the winds and the waves of the sea, as they are carried

116

onward in their courses by the power of the Almighty. Edwards looks for liberty, and he finds it, not in the will, but in the motions of the body, which is universally admitted to be passive to the action of the will. He looks for liberty, and he finds it, where, by universal consent, an absolute necessity reigns; thus seeking and finding the living among the dead. It is no wonder, that he could reconcile such a liberty with the scheme of necessity.

Even President Day is not satisfied with this account of liberty. "On the subject of liberty or freedom," says he, "which occupies a portion of the fifth section of Edwards' first book, he has been less particular than was to be expected, considering that this is the great object of inquiry in his work." How could Edwards have been more particular? He has repeatedly and most explicitly informed us, that liberty consists in a power, or opportunity, to do as we choose; *without considering how we come by our choice.* If we can only do as we choose, though our choice should be produced by the most absolute and irresistible power in the universe, yet are we perfectly free in the highest conceivable sense of the word. "If any imagine they desire, and that they conceive of a higher liberty than this," says he, "they are deceived, and delude themselves with confused ambiguous words instead of ideas." President Day complains that all this is not sufficiently particular; but although he may not have been aware of it, I apprehend that he has been dissatisfied with the dreadful particularity and precision with which the doctrine of the Inquiry has been exhibited. It is precisely the doctrine of liberty which has been held by the most absolute and unqualified fatalists the world has ever seen; and it is set forth, too, with a bold precision and clearness, which would have done honour to the stern consistency of Hobbes himself. It is no wonder, that President Day should have felt a desire to see such a doctrine softened down by the author of the Inquiry.

"The professed object of his book," says President Day, "*according to the title-page,* is an inquiry concerning the freedom of the will;—not the freedom of external conduct. We naturally look for his meaning of this internal liberty. What he has said, in this section, respecting freedom of the will, has rather the appearance of evading such a definition of it as might be considered his own." Yes, it is in this section that we naturally look for his idea of the liberty of the will; but we do not find it. We must turn to the title-page, if we wish to see any thing about the liberty of the will. "What he has said, in this section, respecting freedom of the will," does not, (President Day himself being judge,) relate to the freedom of the will at all; it only relates to the freedom of the body, which has no freedom at all; but which is wholly passive to the action of the will. President Day is not satisfied with all this; and hence, he proceeds to tell us, what Edwards would have said in this section, if he had not thus evaded his own definition of internal liberty. Let us see, then, what he would have said.

From a letter to a minister of the Church of Scotland, President Day finds that in the phrase conducting as a man pleases, the author of the Inquiry means to include the idea of *choosing as he pleases*. Now, this is all true; and this is the internal liberty, which President Day has extracted from the aforesaid letter. Then, according to Edwards, we have two kinds of liberty: the one is a liberty to move the body as we please, or as we choose; and the other is, to choose as we please, or as we choose. In the vocabulary, and according to the psychology of President Edwards, as we have frequently seen, and as we here see, our pleasing and our choosing are one and the same thing. Hence, to move our bodies according to our pleasure, is to move it according to our choice; and to choose as we please, is to choose as we choose. President Day need not have gone to the letter in question, in order to find this doctrine; for it is repeatedly set forth in the inquiry. President Edwards, as we have seen, frequently contends in the Inquiry, that we always choose as we choose; and as frequently makes his adversaries assert, that we can "choose without choosing;" which is just as absurd, he truly declares, as to say that a body can move while it is in a state of rest.

Now, to place liberty in this "choosing as we choose," without regard to the cause or origin of our choice, is just about as rational as it would be to place it in the axioms of geometry. Suppose a man is made to choose, by an absolute and uncontrollable power; it is nevertheless true, that he chooses as he does choose. This cannot be otherwise than true; it is a self-evident and necessary truth; for nothing can be different from itself, can be what it is, and yet not what it is, at one and the same time. To speak of a power of choosing as we choose, as Edwards and Day both do, is just about as reasonable as it were to speak of a power to make two and two equal to four. Supposing the Almighty should cause us to choose, it is not in his power to prevent us from choosing as we do choose; for he cannot work contradictions.

Whether President Edwards speaks of our moving as we please, or of our choosing as we please; whether he speaks of an external liberty, or of this internal liberty; he is always careful to remind us, that it has no reference to the question, how we come by our pleasure or choice. In the letter referred to, wherein he admits that a man's liberty of conducting as he pleases or chooses, includes "a liberty of choosing as he pleases," he instantly adds, but "without determining how he came by that pleasure." Yes, no matter how we come by our choice, though it be wrought into us by the most uncontrollable power in the universe, yet are we free in the highest conceivable sense of the word, if we can only "conduct according to our choice." This, instead of being the greatest liberty, is indeed the greatest mockery, of which it is possible for the imagination of man to conceive. The liberty of fate itself, is, in all respects, to the full as desirable as such a liberty as this. Is it not wonderful, to behold the great and good author of the Inquiry, thus planting himself upon the very ground of atheistical fatalism; and from thence, in sober, serious earnestness, holding out to us, as a great and glorious reality, the mere name and shadow and fiction of liberty? the very phantom which atheists, in mockery and derision, have been pleased to confer upon mankind, as upon poor blind fools, who merely dream of liberty, and fondly dote upon the empty name thereof, whilst they are ignorant of the chains which bind them fast in fate.

SECTION XV.

OF EDWARDS' IDEA OF VIRTUE.

IN order to reconcile his scheme of necessity with the existence and reality of virtue, it appears that Edwards has adopted a false notion of virtue. This is the course he has taken, as I have already shown, in regard to the doctrine of liberty or free-agency, in order to reconcile it with necessity; and if I mistake not, it may be shown, that he has been able to reconcile necessity and virtue only by transforming the nature of virtue to make it suit his system.

I do not intend, at present, to enter into a full discussion of the author's views in relation to the nature of virtue. I shall content myself with a brief consideration of his notion of virtue, as it stands more immediately and directly connected with the subject of the Inquiry.

It is a fundamental principle with him, that "the essence of the virtue and viciousness of dispositions of the heart, and acts of the will, lies not in their cause, but their nature." In what precise sense the author would have us to understand this proposition, I shall not now stop to inquire. It is sufficient for my present purpose, that he attaches such a sense to it, as to make the idea of virtue it is intended to define, to agree not only with his doctrine of necessity, but also with any other kind of necessity or fatality whatever. For he maintains, that as the essence of virtue does not consist in its cause, but in its nature, so a man by the mere act of creation may, in the proper sense of the word, be endowed with virtuous and holy dispositions. It is true, the man himself has had no share in the production of his dispositions, they are exclusively the work of his Creator; but yet they are virtuous, they are the objects of moral approbation, because the virtuousness of dispositions has nothing at all to do with their cause or origin. It depends wholly on their nature, and having this nature, (as he supposes they may have by creation alone,) he concludes that they are properly and truly virtuous, although the person in whom they exist has in no manner whatever contributed to their production; neither in whole nor in part, neither exclusively nor concurrently with his Maker. Now, it is evident, I think, that if virtue may be made to exist in this way, by a power wholly extraneous to the being in whom it exists, and wholly independent of all his own thoughts and reflections and doings, then it may be easily reconciled with the most absolute scheme of fatality that has ever been advocated. For it may exist without any agency or concurrence or consent on the part of the person in whom it exists; and hence, there would be no difficulty in reconciling it with any scheme of necessity that any fatalist may be pleased to advance.

To show that I have not misrepresented the author, I shall select from many passages of similar import, the following from his work on "Original Sin:"—"Human nature must be created with some dispositions; a disposition to relish some things as good and amiable, and to be averse to other things as odious and disagreeable: otherwise it must be without any such thing as inclination or will, perfectly indifferent, without preference, without choice or aversion towards any thing as agreeable or disagreeable. But if it had any concreated dispositions at all, they must be either right or wrong, either agreeable or disagreeable to the nature of things. If man had at first the highest relish of things excellent and beautiful, a disposition to have the quickest and highest delight in those things which are most worthy of it, then his dispositions were morally right and amiable, and *never can be excellent in a higher sense.* But if he had a disposition to love most those things that were inferior and less worthy, then his dispositions were vicious. And it is evident there can be no medium between these."

Now, this principle, that a man may be to praise or to blame, that he may be esteemed virtuous or vicious, on account of what he has wholly and exclusively received from another, appears to me to be utterly irreconcilable with one of the clearest and most unequivocal dictates of reason and conscience.

According to the above passage, there can be no medium between virtuous and vicious dispositions. This sentiment is still more explicitly declared in the following words; "In a moral agent, subject to moral obligations, it is the same thing to be perfectly *innocent*, as to be perfectly *righteous*. It must be the same, because there can no more be any medium between sin and righteousness, or between being right and being wrong, in a moral sense, than there can be between being straight and crooked, in a natural sense." Now, all this is very true, in regard to a moral being who has been called upon to act; for he must either live up to the rule of duty, or he must fall short of it. If he does the former, he becomes righteous in the true and proper sense of the term; and if he does the latter, he loses his original innocence, and becomes a transgressor. But before he has any opportunity of acting, at the instant of his creation, I humbly conceive that no moral agent is either to be praised or blamed for any disposition with which he may have been endowed by his Maker. He is neither virtuous nor vicious, neither righteous nor sinful. This was the condition of Adam, as it very clearly appears to me, at the instant of his creation. He was in a state of perfect *innocency*; having neither transgressed the law of God, nor attained to true holiness. And if this be the case, then in regard to such a moral agent, before he has an opportunity to act, or to think, or to feel, it is not "the same thing to

121

be perfectly innocent, as to be, perfectly righteous;" nor the same thing to be destitute of true righteousness, as to be sinful.

It strikes my mind with the force of a self-evident truth, that nothing can be our virtue, unless we are in some sense the author of it; and to affirm that a man may be justly praised or blamed, that he may be esteemed virtuous or vicious, on account of what he has wholly and exclusively received from another, appears to me to contradict one of the clearest and most unequivocal dictates of reason, one of the most universal and irreversible laws of human belief.

Though the Almighty endowed Adam with all that is lovely in human nature, the recipient of such noble qualities certainly deserved no credit for them, as he had no agency in their production. All the praise and glory belonged to God. Such dispositions are no doubt the objects of our admiration and love, but they are no more the objects of our *moral approbation* than is the beauty of a flower. Both are the work of the same creative energy which hath diffused so much of loveliness and beauty over every part of the creation.

Hence, I deny that Adam was "created or brought into existence righteous." I am willing to admit, that he "was brought into existence capable of acting immediately as a moral agent; and, therefore, he was immediately under a rule of *right* action. He was obliged as soon as he existed, to *act right.*" But I deny that until he did begin to act, he could possess the character of true holiness or virtue. That President Edwards thought otherwise, is evident, not only from the passage already quoted, but also from many others, as well as from the fact, that he argues if Adam had not possessed virtuous dispositions before he began to act,—if he had not derived them directly from his Creator, then the existence of virtue would have been impossible.

On this subject, his argument is ingenious and plausible. It is as follows: "It is agreeable to the sense of men, in all nations and ages, not only that the fruit or effect of a good choice is virtuous, but that the good choice itself from whence that effect proceeds, is so; yea, also the antecedent good disposition, temper, or affection of mind, from whence proceeds that *good* choice, is virtuous. This is the general notion—not that principles derive their goodness from actions, but—that actions derive their goodness from the principles whence they proceed; so that the act of choosing what is good, is no further virtuous, than it proceeds from a good principle, or virtuous disposition of mind. Which supposes that a virtuous disposition of mind, may be before a virtuous act of choice; and that, therefore, it is not necessary there should first be thought, reflection, and choice, before there can be any virtuous disposition. If the choice be first, before the existence of a good disposition of heart, what is the character of that choice? There can, according to our natural notions, be no virtue in a choice which proceeds from no virtuous principle, but from mere self-love, ambition, or some animal appetite: therefore, a virtuous temper of mind may be before a good act of choice, as a tree may be before the fruit, and the fountain before the stream which proceeds from it," p. 407.

It is true, that actions derive their good or evil quality, as the case may be, from the principles whence they proceed. This accords, as the author truly says, with the universal sentiment of mankind. But this proposition, plain and simple as it appears to be at first sight, may be misunderstood. The term "principle" is ambiguous; and, according to the idea attached to it, the above proposition may be true or false. When it is said, for example, that a vicious or sinful action derives its evil quality from the principle or motive whence it proceeds, I apprehend that no one pretends to fix the brand of condemnation on the implanted principle, or the natural spring of action, from which it is supposed to proceed. To take the very case in question; our first parents, in eating the forbidden fruit, acted partly from a desire of food and partly from a desire of knowledge. Now, this was a sinful action, because forbidden, and consequently, according to the sense of men in all ages and nations, it must have proceeded from a sinful inclination or principle. But yet no one, I presume, will contend that either the desire of food or the desire of knowledge, from which it is supposed to have proceeded, is in itself sinful. They were implanted in our nature by the finger of God, for wise and beneficent purposes; and to assert that they are sinful, is to make God the author of sin. Our first parents were not to blame because they were endowed with these principles. Hence, when it is said, that a sinful action must proceed from a sinful principle, we are not to understand the proposition as meaning that the inherent constitutional principle of action from which it is supposed to proceed is sinful. Our first parents sinned, not in possessing an appetite for food, or a desire for knowledge, but in indulging these contrary to the will of God. It was their *intention* and *design* to do that which God had commanded them not to do, and which they knew it was wrong for them to do. It was this intention and design, which was certainly not an implanted principle, or any part of the work of the Creator, which constituted their sin; and it is this intention and design that is pointed at, when it is said, that the principle or motive from which their transgression proceeded, was a sinful principle or motive. And hence, we very clearly perceive, that a sinful action may result from those principles of our constitution, which are in themselves neither virtuous nor vicious, which are wholly destitute of any moral character whatever. So, in like manner, a virtuous action may result from a principle of our nature, implanted in the human breast by the Author of our being, although such principle may not, properly speaking, be called a virtuous principle, or an object of moral approbation.

The fallacy of the author's argument, I conceive, has arisen from the ambiguity of the term principle. As it is truly said, that a holy action can proceed only from a holy principle or disposition, he concluded, that if man had not been created with a principle of virtue or holiness in his heart, then no such thing as virtue or holiness could ever have found its way into the world. Supposing, all the time, that it is universally considered that a virtuous act could proceed only from an implanted principle of virtue, of which God alone is the author; whereas, in fact, the virtuous principle from which the virtuous act is supposed to derive its character, is not an implanted principle at all, but the design, or intention, or motive with which the act is done; and of which the created agent is himself the author.

There is one thing well worthy of remark in this connexion. President Edwards contends, as we have seen, that Adam must have been created with a principle of virtue, of which his Maker was the sole author, or else the existence of virtue would have been impossible, And yet, he contends that Adam was created perfectly free from sin;—that as he came from the hand of his Maker, he was perfectly pure and holy, without the least stain or blemish of any wrong or vicious principle upon his nature. Is it not wonderful, that it did not occur to so acute a reasoner as the author of the "Inquiry," that if his own argument was sound, it would, according to his own principle, prove the introduction of sin into the world to be utterly impossible? That he did not see, if it is impossible to account for the existence of holiness, except on the supposition that man was created or brought into the world with a principle of holiness implanted in his heart; so, for the same reason, it is equally impossible to account for the existence of sin, except on the supposition that a sinful principle was implanted in the breast of man by the hand of his Maker?

The above extract, by which Edwards endeavours to prove that Adam could not have performed a virtuous act, unless a virtuous principle had been planted in his nature by the Creator, would be just as correct and conclusive, if we were to read vicious instead of virtuous. By the very same argument, we might prove that he could not have sinned, and so sin would have been impossible, unless God had planted a sinful principle or disposition in his nature.

It is sufficiently evident, that President Edwards' idea of the essence of virtue, was not altogether correct, and that he was led to adopt it by the necessities of a false system. For if we admit that the essence of virtue or of sin consists in its nature, and not in its cause or origin, it must be conceded, on the other hand, that the nature of those principles, or dispositions, or volitions, or habits, (call them what we may,) which are termed virtuous or vicious, depend in a very important sense upon their cause or origin. It must be conceded, that no disposition or principle whatever which has derived its origin wholly from any cause or power extraneous to the moral agent in which it exists, can be properly denominated virtuous or vicious. It cannot partake of the nature of virtue or of vice, unless it owes its origin to the agent whose virtue or whose vice it is supposed to be. If it proceeds wholly from the "power, influence, or action," of motives, or from the hand of the Creator, it is not the act of the agent in whom it exists, and consequently he is not accountable for it. Or, in other words, the nature of virtue and vice is such, that they cannot possibly be produced by any "cause, or power, or influence," which is wholly extraneous to the mind in which they exist. Virtue and vice, in the strict and proper sense of the words, must have the concurrence and consent of the mind in which they exist, or they cannot possibly exist at all. To speak of virtue,—of that which deserves our moral approbation, as being wholly derived from another—as being exclusively the work of God in the soul, is to be guilty of a contradiction, as plain and palpable as the light of heaven. It is to be regretted, it is to be deeply lamented, that Edwards did not try to bring his doctrine of the will into harmony with the common sentiments of mankind with respect to the nature of virtue and free-agency, instead of exerting his matchless powers to make virtue and free-agency agree with his scheme of necessity, by explaining away and transforming their natures. It is to be lamented; because in attempting to uphold and support the distinctive peculiarities of his own system of theology, he has unintentionally struck a deadly blow at the vital and fundamental principles of all religion, both natural and revealed. The infidel and the atheist are much indebted to him for such an exertion of his immortal powers.

SECTION XVI.

OF THE SELF-DETERMINING POWER.

THE advocates of free-agency have contended that the will is determined by itself, and not by the strongest motive. This is the ground which, so far as I know, has always been taken against the doctrine of necessity; but it may be questioned whether it is tenable, and whether the friends of moral agency might not have made far greater headway against their adversaries if they had not assumed such a position. It appears to be involved in several inevitable contradictions; in the exposure of which the necessitarian has been accustomed to triumph.

The leading argument of Edwards against the self-determining power may be substantially stated in a few words. The will can be the cause of no effect, says he, except by acting, or putting forth a volition to cause it; and hence, if we assert that the will causes its own volitions, we must suppose it causes them by preceding volitions. It can cause a volition only by a prior volition, which, in its turn, can be caused only by another volition prior to it; and so on *ad infinitum*. Thus, according to Edwards, the self-determining power of the will necessarily runs out into the absurdity of an infinite series of volitions.

If this reasoning is just, the doctrine in question must be abandoned; for no sound doctrine can lead to such a conclusion. But is it just? Does such an absurdity really flow from the self-determining power of the will?

It has been objected to the argument of Edwards, that it is based on a false assumption. The position of Edwards, "that if the will determines itself, it must determine itself by an act of choice," is, it has been contended, clearly an assumption unsupported, and incapable of being supported. The reason assigned for this objection is, that we do not know how any cause exerts itself in the production of phenomena; and consequently we have no right to assume that the will can cause its volitions only by volitions. In other words, as we do not know how any cause produces its effects, so it is wholly a gratuitous assumption to say, that if the will causes its volitions, it must cause them in this particular manner, that is, by preceding acts of volition.

This objection does not seem to be well taken. When we say, that the will is the cause of any thing, we do not really mean that the will itself is the cause of it; for the will itself does not act: it is not an agent, it is merely the power of an agent. It is that power by which the mind acts. Hence, when the will is said to cause a thing, the language must either have no intelligible meaning, or it must be understood to mean, that the mind causes it by an exercise of its power of willing. But to say that the mind causes a thing by an exercise of its

126

power of willing, is to say that it causes it by an act of the will or a volition; which brings us to the assumption of Edwards. Hence, if the language that "the will causes its own volitions" means any thing, it must mean what Edwards supposes it does. That is, if the will causes its volition, or rather, if the mind in the act of willing causes them, then they must be caused by volitions or acts of the will.

It is said, that "we do not know *how* any cause acts." This is very true, when properly understood; but in the true sense of this maxim, Edwards has not undertaken to explain how a cause acts; nor has he made any assumption as to how it acts. The *term* cause has a variety of meanings; and it is frequently applied with extreme vagueness and want of precision. What is the cause of an effect?—of the motion of the hand, for example? It is the mind, says one; it is the will, says another; it is a volition, replies a third. Now here are three distinct things,—the mind, the will, and the volition; and yet each is said to be the cause of the same identical effect. This diversity of expression may do very well in popular discourse, but it must be laid aside whenever philosophical precision is required.

What is then, really and properly speaking, the cause of the motion in question? It is neither the mind, nor the will; for these might both exist, and yet no such effect result from them. A mind, or a will, that lies still and does not act, is the cause of no effect. If we would speak with philosophical precision, then, we should say that the act of the mind is the cause of the effect in question. The idea of a cause, in the strict and proper sense of the term, is that from which the effect immediately and necessarily flows. Now the motion of the hand is not necessarily connected with the mind itself; for if the mind were to lie still and not act, no such effect would follow. It is with the act of the mind that the effect in question is connected as with its efficient cause. It is the act of the mind which implies the motion of the hand, and that is implied by it; and hence, it is the act of the mind, or the volition, that is properly said to be the cause of such motion. For cause and effect, are said to imply each other.

Now Edwards has not pretended to say how a volition acts upon the external part of our being; if he had done so, he would have been justly obnoxious to the charge of presuming to know how a cause acts, in the proper sense of the word; but he has done no such thing. The connexion between cause and effect, in the proper sense of the terms, he has left enveloped in profound mystery. He has not presumed to say how an act, or cause, properly so called, produces its corresponding effect.

He does not assume to know how a cause acts; but how what is sometimes called a cause really becomes such. The will may be called a cause, if you please; but, in reality, unless it acts, it is the cause of no effect; and even then, properly speaking, the act is the cause. He clearly saw that a will which lies still and does nothing, is the cause of no effect; and hence he stated the simple fact, that it must act in order to become a cause, or, which is the same thing, in order to produce an effect. And is not this perfectly self-evident? We do not know how the will acts, nor how its act produces a change in the external part of our being; but yet do we not certainly know, that a dormant will can do nothing, and that it must act in order to produce an effect. If this be to explain how a cause acts, I humbly conceive that we may do so with perfect propriety.

Indeed, all that is assumed by Edwards, has been conceded to him by most of his adversaries. Thus says Dr. West, as quoted by Edwards the younger, "No being can become a cause, i. e. an efficient, or that which produces an effect, but by first operating, acting, or energizing." Here we are told, not how a cause acts, but how the mind becomes a cause, or the author of effects. This is all that Edwards takes for granted; and, for aught that I can see, he has done so with perfect propriety.

The same thing is conceded by Dr. Reid. "The change," says he, "whether it be of thought, of will, or of motion, is the effect. Active power, therefore, is a quality in the cause, which enables it to produce the effect. And the exertion of that active power in producing the effect, is called action, agency, efficiency. In order to the production of any effect, there must be in the cause, not only power, *but the exertion of that power.*"—Essays on the Active Powers, p. 259. Here it is declared by Dr. Reid, that active power or the will must act, in order to produce an effect, whether the effect be in the mind itself, or out of the mind, whether it be "of thought, of will, or of motion." This is all that Edwards assumes as the basis of his argument.

But the question is not so much what has been conceded, as what is true. Is it true, then, that if the will causes its own volitions, it can cause them only by preceding volitions? It is, as we have already seen, according to the common acceptation of the terms; for a dormant cause can produce no effect; it must act in order to produce effects. Edwards has truly said, that "if the will be determined, there is a determiner. This must be supposed to be intended even by those that say the will determines itself. If it be so, the will is both determiner and determined; it is a cause that acts and produces effects upon itself, and is the object of its own influence and action." p. 19. Now, whatever may be the meaning of those who choose to affirm that the will determines itself, admitting that it is both determined and determiner; the conclusion of

Edwards seems to be fairly drawn from the language in which their doctrine is expressed. To say the least, he fairly reduces the obvious meaning of their language to the absurdity of an infinite series of volitions.

If the phrase, that the will is determined by itself, has any meaning, it must mean, either that the will is made to act by a preceding act of the will, or that the will simply acts. If the meaning be, that the act or choice of the will is produced by a preceding act of the will, then is the inference of Edwards well drawn, and the self-determining power is involved in the aforesaid *ad infinitum* absurdity. But if the meaning be, that the will simply acts, why not present the idea in this its true and unambiguous form?

It is evident, that while the will remains inactive, it can produce no effect; it must act, in order to become the author of effects. The effect caused, and the causative act, are clearly distinct; the one produces the other. If the causative act is a volition, then we have an infinite series of volitions. And if it be not a volition, but some other effort of the mind, the same difficulty arises; for if it be necessary to suppose a preceding effort of the mind in order to account for a volition, it will be equally necessary to suppose the existence of another effort to account for that; and so on *ad infinitum*. And an infinite series of efforts is just as great an absurdity as an infinite series of volitions.

Now let us suppose that, in order to escape these difficulties, an advocate of the self-determining power should deny that there is any causative act of volition; but that volition is itself an act uncaused by any preceding act. According to this view, what does the self-determining power amount to? It amounts to just this, that the will itself acts,—a position which is as freely recognized by Edwards as it could possibly be by the warmest advocate of the self-determining power. If this be all that is meant by self-determination, why not state the simple fact that the will itself acts, in plain English, instead of going about to envelope it in a mist of words? If this be all that is meant, why not state the thing so that it may be acquiesced in by the necessitarian, instead of keeping up such a war of words? Indeed, it appears plain to me, that the assertion that the will is determined by itself, is either false doctrine, or else the language in which it is couched is not a clear and distinct expression of its own meaning. On either supposition, this mode of expression should be abandoned.

I have long been impressed with the conviction, that the self-determining power, as it is generally understood, is full of inconsistencies. While we hold this doctrine, we cannot with a good grace contend that the motive-determining power is involved in the absurdity of an infinite series of causes;

for we ourselves are involved in it. Nor can we very well maintain that "a necessary agent is no agent at all;" for the necessitarian will reply, as he always does, that according to our own scheme, our actions are caused; and hence, if it be absurd to speak of a caused action, this is equally true, whether the cause be intrinsic or extrinsic. Moreover, if we should complain that, according to the necessitarian, the phenomena of the will are involved in the "mechanism of cause and effect," he will be sure to reply, that the same thing is true according to our own scheme, inasmuch as we admit volition to be an effect, and place it under the dominion of an internal cause. These difficulties, as well as some others, have always encumbered the cause of free and accountable agency; just because it has been supposed to consist in the self-determining power of the will. We should, therefore, abandon this doctrine. If Clarke, and Price, and Reid, and West, have not been able to maintain it without running into such inconsistencies, it is high time it should be laid aside forever.

It has always been taken for granted that the will is determined. The use of this word clearly implies that the will is acted upon, either by the will itself, or by something else. It has been conceded, on all sides, that it is determined; and the only controversy has been, as to what is the determiner. It is determined by the strongest motive, says one; it is determined by itself, says another; and upon these two positions the combatants have arranged themselves. But behind all this controversy, there is a question which has not been agitated; and that is, whether the will is determined at all? For my part, I am firmly and fully persuaded that it is not, but that it simply determines. It is the "determiner," but not the "determined." It is never the object of its own determination. It acts, but there is no causative act, by which it is made to act. This position, I trust, has been made good in the preceding pages.

If we say that the will is determined by itself, this implies that it is determined in the passive voice, at the same time that it determines in the active voice; whereas, in reality, it is simply active, and not passive to the action of any thing, in its determinations. We should not say, then, that the mind is self-determined, but simply that it is self-active. On this ground we may securely rest in our opposition to the scheme of necessity. It can never be shown that it is involved in the absurdity of an endless series of causes; it will remain for the necessitarian alone to extricate himself from that absurdity. That the mind is self-active, I have already shown, by showing that it is absurd to suppose that an act of the mind is produced by the action of any thing upon it. It is right here, then, upon the self-activity of the human mind, that we take our stand, in order to plant the lever which shall heave the scheme of moral necessity from its foundations. It is right here that we find our stronghold; that we erect the bulwark and the fortifications of man's free-agency, against which, as against a wall of adamant, all the shafts of the necessitarian will fall blunted to the earth, or else recoil with destructive force upon himself.

But why fight against the doctrine of those who have laboured in the same great cause with myself? Truly, most truly, not because it is a grateful task, but because it is a deep and earnest conviction, wrought into my mind by the meditation of years, that the great and glorious cause of free-agency has been retarded by some of the errors of its friends, more than by all the truths of its enemies. This has appeared to be the case especially in regard to the self-determining power of the will. It seems to have retained its hold upon the mind of its friends, not so much by its intrinsic merits, as by its denial of moral necessity, and the idea that it is the only mode of such denial. As the scheme of moral necessity has triumphed in the weakness of the self-determining power, so has the self-determining power resisted the siege of centuries, in the unconquerable energy of its opposition to the determining and controlling power of motives. And if both have stood together, each deriving strength from the weakness of the other, is it not possible that both may fall together, and that a more complete and satisfactory scheme of moral agency may arise out of the common ruins?

SECTION XVII.

OF THE DEFINITION OF A FREE AGENT.

HAVING shown, as I trust, that there is no influence whatever operating upon the mind to produce volition, I am now prepared to declare the true idea of a free-agent.

A free-agent, then, is one who acts without being caused to act. Here the question arises, Is such a thing possible? Can any being act, without being caused to act? The answer to this question, depends upon the meaning which is attached to the very ambiguous term cause. If it means an efficient cause, or that which produces a thing by prior action or influence, it is possible for a spirit to act without being caused to do so; and, as we have already seen, if there can be no action without such a cause of its existence, then there must be an infinite series of actions or causes. But if the question be, Can an act arise and come into being, without a sufficient "ground and reason" of its existence? I answer, No. It is very necessary to separate the different questions included in the general one, Is not a volition caused? or has it not a cause? and to pass upon them separately.

There is, I admit, a "sufficient ground and reason" for our actions; but not an *efficient* cause of them. This is the all-important distinction which has been overlooked in the present controversy. Edwards frequently asks, if a volition is without a cause? Now we call for a division of this question. Has volition an efficient cause? I answer, No. Has it a "sufficient ground and reason" of its existence? I answer, Yes. No one ever imagined that there are no indispensable antecedents to choice, without which it could not take place; but Edwards has framed this question in such a manner, that we cannot give a categorical answer to it, without either denying our own doctrine, or else subscribing to his. Unless there were a mind, there could be no act of the mind; and unless the mind possessed a power of acting, it could not put forth volitions. The mind, then, and the power of the mind called will, constitute the ground of action or volition.

But a power to act, it will be said, is not a sufficient reason to account for the existence of action. This is true. The *reason* is to come. The sufficient reason, however, is not an efficient cause; for there is some difference between a blind impulse or force, and rationality. The mind is endowed with various appetites, passions, and desires,—with noble affections, and, above all, with a feeling of moral approbation and disapprobation. These are not the "active principles," or the "motive powers," as they have been called; they are the ends of our acting: we simply act in order to gratify them. They exert no

132

influence over the will, much less is the will controlled by them; and hence, we are perfectly free, to gratify the one or the other of them;—to act in obedience to the dictates of conscience, or in order to gratify the lowest appetites of our nature. We see that certain means must be used, in order to gratify the passion, desire, affection, or feeling, which we *intend* to gratify; and we act accordingly. In all this, we form our designs or *intentions* free from all influence whatever: nothing acts upon the will: we fix upon the end, and we choose the means to accomplish it. We adapt the means to our end; because there is a fitness in them to accomplish that end or design; and because, as rational creatures, we perceive that fitness. Thus, we act according to reason, but not from the influence of reason. We act with a view to our desires, but not from the influence of our desires; and our volition is virtuous or vicious according to the intention with which it is put forth,—according to the design with which it is directed. Passion is not "the gale," it is "the card." Reason is not the force, it is the law. All the power resides in the free, untrammelled will. He who overlooks this, and blindly seeks for something to "move the mind to volition," loses sight of the grand and distinctive peculiarity of man's nature, and brings it down to the dust, subjecting it to the laws of matter and to bondage.

We do not allow Mr. Hobbes to declare our idea of a free-agent, as "one that, when all the circumstances necessary to produce action are present, *can nevertheless not act;*" nor do we accept of the amendment, of another, "that a free-agent is one who, when all the circumstances necessary to produce action are present, *can act.*" For if all the circumstances necessary *to produce* action are present, then they would produce it; and nothing would be left for the will to do, except to receive the producing influence. In other words, if volition is produced by circumstances, then it is a passive impression made upon the will, and not an act at all.

It is contended by Edwards, that it is just as absurd to say, that a volition can come into existence without a cause, as it is that a world should do so. It is true, that a world cannot arise out of nothing, and come into existence of itself; and this is also equally true of a volition. But is the mind nothing? Is the will nothing? Is a free, intelligent, designing cause nothing?

The mind is something; and it is capable of acting in order to fulfil its own designs, though it be not impelled to act. Is this idea absurd? Is it self-contradictory? Is it any thing like the assertion, that an effect has no cause? It is not. It implies no contradiction;—it is a possible idea. How does it act, then? I do not know. This is a mystery. Indeed, every ultimate fact in man's nature, and every simple exercise of his intellectual powers, is a mystery. An exercise of the power of conception, by which the past is called up, and made to pass in review before us; an exercise of the imagination, by which the world is made to teem with wonders of our own creation; and an exercise of the will, by which we produce changes in, the external world; are all mysteries? Now, shall we fly from these mysteries? Shall we strive to make the matter plain, in a single instance, by assigning an efficient cause to an act of the will? If so, whether we escape the *mystery* or not, we shall certainly plunge into *absurdity*. We shall embrace a doctrine, which denies the nature of action, and which is necessarily involved in the great absurdity of an infinite series of causes. For my part, I prefer a simple statement of the fact of volition, with its attendant circumstances, how much soever of mystery it may seem to leave around the subject, to any *explanation* which involves it in absurdity.

The philosophers of all ages have sought for the efficient cause of volition; but who has found it? Is it in the will? The necessitarian has shown the absurdities of this hypothesis. Is it in the power of motive? This hypothesis is fraught with the very same absurdities. Is it in the uncaused volition of Deity? The younger Edwards could do nothing with this hypothesis. In truth, the efficient cause of volition is nowhere. It has never been found, because it does not exist; and it never will be found, so long as an action of mind continues to be what it is.

This, then, is the true idea of a free-agent: it is one who, in view of circumstances, both external and internal, can act, without being efficiently caused to do so. This is the idea of a free-agent which God has realized by the creation of the soul of man. It may be a mystery; but it is not a contradiction. It may be a mystery; but then it solves a thousand difficulties which we have unnecessarily created to ourselves. It may be a mystery; but then it is the only safe retreat from self-contradiction, absurdity, and atheism.

It is no reason for disbelieving a thing, that we cannot conceive how it is. This will be readily admitted; but this principle, like every other, may be misapplied and abused. If any thing is possible in itself considered, that is, if it implies no contradiction, we should not refuse to believe it, because we cannot conceive how it is. When confined within these limits, the principle or maxim in question is one of immense importance; and to disregard it betrays one of the greatest weaknesses to which the human mind is exposed. If we do not adhere to it, there is no resting-place for us this side of the most unqualified atheism: we shall be compelled to renounce, not only the stupendous facts and mysteries of revelation, but also all the great truths of natural religion. The very being and attributes of God can find no place in our minds, if we expunge this principle from them; and insist upon seeing how every thing is, before we consent to receive it as an object of belief.

We should find no difficulty, therefore, in believing that the mind of man acts, without being efficiently caused to act. This implies no contradiction; and hence the creative power of God can produce such a being—a being that acts freely, without labouring under any necessity, either natural or moral, in its accountable and moral agency. A being, the end of whose action is found in the sensibility; the intention, the design, and the plan of whose action is formed in the intelligence; and the power by which this intention is executed, and this plan accomplished, is in the will alone. It is in this triunity of the sensibility, the intelligence, and the will, that the glory of man's nature, as a free and accountable being, consists. The relation between them is most intimate,—is inconceivably intimate; but the relation is not the same in nature and kind as that which subsists between an effect and its efficient, or producing cause. The only relation of this kind, which is to be found in the case, is that which subsists between the action of the will, or the volition, and the corresponding change which it produces in the external part of our being. I say, we can very easily believe all this, as it implies no contradiction; and yet not feel ourselves bound, by a regard for consistency, to believe that a world may rise up out of nothing, and come into being of itself, without any cause of its existence. These things are blended together, in the philosophy of the necessitarian, by a most convenient use of an ambiguous phraseology; but they are, indeed, as widely different from each other as mystery is from absurdity,—as light is from darkness.

But the above maxim, as I have already said, may be grievously misapplied; and thus the garb of intellectual humility may be thrown over the greatest absurdities. We may be told, for example, that the same body may be wholly in one place, and wholly in a far distant place, at one and the same time; and, if we object to this doctrine, the murmurings of reason are sought to be silenced, by reminding us, that it is exceedingly weak and presumptuous for poor blind creatures like ourselves, to reject a truth because we cannot conceive how it is. In like manner, we are informed that a volition, or an act of the will, may be produced in the mind, may be necessitated, by the action of an extraneous cause; or, if you please, of an intrinsic cause; and if we ask how this can be, without interfering with our free-agency, it is frequently replied, that we cannot tell; but that it is exceedingly absurd and presumptuous to disbelieve a thing because we cannot conceive how it is. That God operates upon the mind, not to rectify and elevate its powers, but to produce a volition in it; not to cleanse and purify the whole stream and current of our natures, but merely to throw up a bubble upon the surface

135

thereof, for which *effect* he holds us accountable: that he does this, we are told, is a great mystery, which we should not presume to call in question. For my part, I had rather believe the doctrine of transubstantiation itself, than such a *mystery* as this.

There is some difference, I have supposed, between disbelieving a thing because we cannot see how it is, and disbelieving it, because we very clearly see that it cannot possibly be any how at all. It is upon this distinction that I stand, when I receive the great mysteries of the Godhead, and reject the absurdities of transubstantiation. And it is upon the same ground, that I most freely and fully recognize and embrace the great mysteries of our being, whilst I reject the absurdities of an efficiently caused and accountable agency.

Is not this distinction properly applied? If the action or influence of any thing produces an effect upon the mind, is not that effect merely a passive impression? Is it not absurd to suppose, that it is a passive impression, produced by the action of something else, and yet that it is an action of the mind itself? If so; and so I think it has been made to appear, then we not only should, but must, reject it. We must reject it, unless we suffer ourselves to be blinded by false analogies, and verbal ambiguities.

This is not to deny the divine influence, as has been so often imagined. The regeneration, the new creation, of the soul, by the power of God, is no more inconsistent with free and accountable agency, than was the original creation of it with all its powers; but this cannot be said of the production of our acts or volitions by a divine influence. Those must take an exceedingly narrow and superficial view of the great work of regeneration; who suppose that it is altogether denied, unless we admit that the Spirit produces our volitions; who suppose that the divine agency can in no way cleanse and purify our powers, unless it can superinduce a volition, or an act, upon our depraved natures. How many persons have laboured in vain, to reconcile the free-agency of man with the reality of a divine influence; just because they have laboured under the superficial notion, the grand illusion, that the Spirit of God cannot act upon the mind at all, unless it acts to produce a volition! It is no wonder that they have laboured in vain, and abandoned the task in despair; because what they have taken for a seeming difficulty, is, when narrowly inspected, seen to be a real absurdity. Lay this aside, and there will be a mystery in the case, it is true; but there will not be *even a seeming contradiction*.

But I do not intend to enter upon the subject of theology. This is entirely beside the purpose of the present work; and if I have touched upon it for a moment, it was only to show, by a passing glance, how very easy it were for any one, if he were so disposed, to draw false conclusions with respect to theology, from the views which have been advanced in regard to the philosophy of the will. True, philosophy and religion will always perfectly harmonize; but then he is very apt to be a poor philosopher, who derives his philosophy from his religion; and he a miserable theologian, who derives his religion from his philosophy. It was in that way, that Edwards became a necessitarian; it is in this, that many a necessitarian has become an infidel or an atheist.

SECTION XVIII.

OF THE TESTIMONY OF CONSCIOUSNESS.

WHETHER our volitions come to pass in the manner we call freely, or are brought to pass by the operation of necessary causes, is a question of fact, which should be referred to the tribunal of consciousness. If we ever hope to settle this question, we must occasionally turn from the arena of dialectics, and unite our efforts in the cultivation of the much-neglected field of observation. We must turn from the dust and smoke of mere logical contention, and consult the living oracle within; we must behold the pure light that ever burns behind the darkened veil of disputation.

This appeal is not declined by the necessitarian. He consents to the appeal; and the dispute is, as to the true interpretation of the decision of the tribunal in question. We contend that the testimony of consciousness is clearly and unequivocally in favour of the doctrine of liberty, while our opponents allege the same evidence in their own favour. Now, what is the real import of this testimony?

It is to be regretted that President Edwards has said so little on this subject. He has disposed of it in one brief note; as if the nature of our mental operations were to be determined by abstract and universal propositions, or truisms, and observation consulted only to confirm our preconceived opinions. What little he has said on this subject, however, is sufficient to show with what faint hope of success the necessitarian can venture to submit his cause to the tribunal of consciousness.

The testimony of consciousness, I have no doubt, might have been made much stronger in our favour, if the wrong question had not been submitted to it. All the advocates of free-agency, so far as I remember, have said that we are conscious of freedom; that we are conscious of a power of contrary choice. Or, in other words, that when we put forth a volition, we are conscious that we might forbear to do so. But this does not seem to be the case. We are not conscious of what does not take place in our minds; and hence, we are only conscious of the volition which we put forth. We are not even conscious of our power to act; this is necessarily inferred from the acts of which we are conscious. As we do not then, according to the supposition, put forth the contrary choice, we cannot be conscious of it, nor of the power to put it forth. By referring this, therefore, to the tribunal of consciousness, it seems to me that most advocates of free-agency have rendered a disservice to the cause which they have so ably supported in other respects. For the necessitarian sees, that the doctrine of liberty, or the power of choice to the contrary, cannot

138

be established by the direct testimony of consciousness alone; and hence he strengthens himself in his own convictions, by picking flaws in our evidence. He sees that we are not borne out by the testimony of consciousness, in regard to the point which we submit to it; and hence, he readily concludes that we are wrong in the whole matter. It is well, it is exceedingly important, to observe what are the strong points of our cause, upon which we can rest with unshaken confidence, and to take our stand upon them; giving up all untenable positions.

By consciousness, then, we discover the existence of an act. We see no cause by which it is produced. If it were produced by the act or operation of any thing else, it would be a passive impression, and not an act of the mind itself. The mind would be wholly passive in relation to it, and it would not be an act at all. Whether it is produced by a preceding act of the mind, or by the action of any thing else, the mind would be passive as to the effect produced. But we see, in the clear and unquestionable light of consciousness, that instead of being passive, the mind is active in its volitions.—Hence, it follows by an inference as clear as noonday, and as irresistible as fate, that the action of the mind is not a produced effect. It is not a passive impression; and hence it does not, *it cannot*, result from the action of any thing else. To say that it is produced by the action of something else upon the mind, is to say that it is a passive impression, and to deny that it is an act. We are simply conscious of an act then, and the irresistible inference which results from this fact, stands out in direct and eternal opposition to the doctrine of necessity.

When we reflect upon the operation of the will, or of the mind in the act of willing, we simply find ourselves in possession of a volition. We do not see how we come by this volition; how we come to exist in this state of activity. On this point, I am happy to find that the consciousness of President Edwards agreed with my own. "It is true," says he, "I find myself possessed of my volitions before I can see the effectual power of any cause to produce them, for the power and efficacy of the cause is seen but by the *effect*, and this, for aught I know, may make some imagine that volition has no cause, or that it produces itself."

Our consciousness is precisely the same; but just observe how he interprets it. He finds himself possessed of a *volition*; but does he look at this volition to see what it is? Does he ask himself whether it is the same in nature and in kind with a produced effect? He does not. It is most unquestionably a produced effect; this is beyond all doubt, and it is taken for granted. He sees no effectual power by which this volition is produced; *but he knows it is a produced effect*, and therefore he knows it must have a producing cause. The oracle is not consulted on this point at all. It would be an insult to reason to consult the great oracle of nature on so plain a point as this. This has been decided long ago, and the ear is deaf to any response that might possibly contravene so clear a decision. Thus it is that the necessitarian goes to the true oracle within, and delivers oracles himself.

He reasons not from the observed, but from the assumed, nature of a volition. It must be an effect, says he, and though I do not see "the effectual power by which it is produced;" yet there must be such a power. Yes, it is just as absurd to suppose that it can exist, without being produced by the effectual power of something operating upon the mind, as it is to suppose that a world can create itself!

But as we appeal to consciousness, let us pay some little attention to its teaching. We find ourselves, then, possessed of a volition; we find our minds in a state of acting. This is all we discover by the light of consciousness. We see "not the effectual power of any cause" operating to produce it. What shall we conclude then? Shall we conclude that there *must* be some cause to produce it? This were not to study nature, as "the humble servants and interpreters thereof;" but to approach it in the attitude of dictators.

If we draw such an inference at all, it must be from the fact, it seems, that volition is a produced effect. But is it such an effect? What says consciousness upon this point? We have already repeatedly seen, what every man may see, that a volition is not the passive result of any prior action; it is action itself. It is not a produced effect; it is a producing cause. It is not *determined* at all; it is simply a *determination*. As it stands out in the light of consciousness, it is as perfectly distinct from the idea of an effect, as any one thing can possibly be from another; and if it has not so appeared to every reflecting mind, it is because it has not been simply looked at, and beheld as it is in itself, but has been viewed through the medium of a certain fixed notion, a certain preconceived form of thought, a certain grand illusion, by which the witchery of the senses has blinded the eye of consciousness. Every change in the external world requires a producing cause; who then can possibly conceive of a volition as existing upon any other terms or conditions! It is this fallacy, this begging of the question, this perpetual declaration that it is self-evident, that has, through a natural illusion of the senses, spread the scheme of necessity far and wide over the minds of men. It is this grand illusion of the senses, or, if you please, of the mind, that has brought "the dictates of reason," as they have been called, into conflict with the testimony of consciousness.

The doctrine of liberty is as inevitably connected with the *observed* nature of a volition, as that of necessity is connected with its assumed nature. I would not say that we are conscious of liberty; for that would not be correct; but I will say, that we are conscious of that which necessarily leads to the conviction that we are free, that we have a power of contrary choice. I would not say with Dr. Clarke, that liberty consists in a power to act; but I will say, that it necessarily results from it. I would not say, that we are conscious of the existence of no producing cause of our volitions; for we cannot be conscious of that which does not exist. But I will say, that as we are conscious of the existence of an act, so we see and do know that this is not a passive impression, or a produced effect. And as we are not compelled to act, so we know that we may act or may not act, so we know that our actions are not necessitated, but may be put forth or withheld. This is liberty, this is "a power of contrary choice." This idea of liberty, I say, follows from the fact of consciousness that we do act, by an inference as clear as noonday; by an inference so natural, so direct, and so inconceivably rapid, that it has often been supposed to be included in the testimony of consciousness itself. No man could help the conclusion, if he would only allow his reason to speak for itself.

Is this doctrine any the less certain, because it is a matter of inference? It will be conceded that it is not. The most unquestionable facts in the universe are made known by the same kind of evidence. It is sometimes said, that we are conscious of our own existence; but this is not to use language with philosophical precision. We are merely conscious of the existence of thought, of feeling, of volition; and we are so made, that we are compelled to believe that there is something which thinks, and feels, and wills. It is thus, by what has been called a fundamental law of belief, that we arrive at the knowledge of the existence of our minds. In like manner, from the fact of consciousness that we do act, or put forth volitions, we are forced, by a fundamental law of belief, to yield to the conviction that we are free. This inference as necessarily results from the observed phenomena of the mind, as the existence of the mind itself results from the same phenomena. And if the doctrine of the necessitarian were true, that volition is a produced effect, we should never infer from it that we have *a power of acting* at all; we should simply infer that we are *susceptible of passive impressions*.

I have said, that we are not conscious that there is no producing cause of volition. No man can be conscious of that which does not exist. Hence, it is highly absurd to require us to furnish the evidence of consciousness that there is no such cause of volition. It cannot testify to any such universal negative; and one might as well require a mathematical demonstration of the point in dispute, as to demand such evidence from us. And yet, President Edwards declares, that by experience he knows nothing like the doctrine, that "any volition arises in his mind contingently;" that is to say, he was not conscious that a volition has *no producing* cause of its existence. Did he expect that we should prove the non-existence of a thing by the direct evidence of consciousness? All that he could reasonably expect in such a case is, that we should not be conscious of any such influence; and this President Edwards himself admits. He admits, that we do not see the "effectual power of any cause," or feel its influence, operating to produce a volition: he merely infers this from the assumption that volition is a produced effect.

He also says, I find "that the acts of my will are my own; i. e. that they are acts of my will—the volitions of my own mind; or, in other words, that what I will, I will; which, I suppose, is the sum of what others experience in this affair." Surely, no one was ever so silly as to deny that what a man wills, he wills; and if this is all that consciousness teaches on the subject, its information can throw no light upon this or upon any other controversy. This proposition, that a man wills what he wills, is independent of all experience and all consciousness. It is an identical proposition, which experience can neither shake nor confirm. We may see, nay, we must see, that each and every thing in the universe is what it is, without any reference to consciousness or experience.

Indeed, it is as absurd to appeal to experience or consciousness for the truth of such a universal and self-evident axiom, as it is to appeal to universal and self-evident axioms, to ascertain and determine the *nature* of our mental phenomena,—of the states and processes of the mind. Edwards has done both: he has deduced the truth of the proposition, that a man wills what he wills, from the evidence of consciousness or experience, as the sum of all its teaching; and he has established the fact, that a volition is produced by the operation of an effectual power, by an appeal to a universal axiom. He has submitted a truism, which declines every test of its truth, to the tribunal of consciousness; and he has determined the nature of a volition, as well as the manner of its production, by the application of a similar truism, which contains no conceivable information respecting the nature of any thing in the universe.

Edwards says, "I find myself possessed of my volitions." He was conscious of his own acts. This is a sufficient foundation for the doctrine of liberty; for such a consciousness is utterly irreconcilable with the supposition that those acts are produced by the operation of efficient causes. To say that they are "my acts," and yet to say that they are produced by the action of

142

something else, is, as we have repeatedly seen, to say that they are my acts, and at the same time to say that they are not my *acts*, but *effects* produced upon my mind. This very admission, therefore, lays the foundation of the doctrine of liberty. And hence, it has been supposed that Edwards himself was an advocate of this doctrine; because he has spoken of the soul as exerting its own volitions. From such an admission, it has been concluded by some of his admirers, that he really regarded the mind as the "efficient cause of its own acts," and "motives as merely the occasions on which it acts." But such an admission only proves, that his consciousness cannot be reconciled with his theory. His consciousness lays the foundation of liberty; but he does not build thereon. On the contrary, he lays the foundation of his system in universal abstractions, and not in observed facts; and hence, as it is not derived from an observation of nature, so it can never be brought into harmony with the dictates and operations of nature. It is altogether a thing of definitions and words; and as such it must pass away, when men shall cease to construct for themselves, and come forward as "the humble servants and interpreters of nature," to study the world of mind upon the true principles of the inductive method.

Edwards did not observe the intellectual world just as it has been constructed by the Almighty, and narrowly watch it in its workings; he only reasoned about it and about it; and hence, he was necessarily devoted to blindness. With all his gigantic power, he was necessarily compelled to go around, eternally, upon the treadmill of a merely dialectical philosophy, which of itself can yield no fruit, instead of going forth to the harvest upon the rich and boundless field of discovery. Why should the failure of other times, resulting from such a course, inspire us with despair? We hope for better results, not from better minds, but from better methods. Socrates dissuaded the men of his time from the study of nature, alleging that "the wonderful art" wherewith the heavens had been constructed, was concealed from their eyes; and that it was displeasing to the gods, that men should so vainly strive to pry into mysteries which are so far above their reach. Faint-hearted sage! Though Bacon had beheld the genius and labour of two thousand years after Socrates had been laid in the dust, wasted upon the same great problem, yet did not the unconquerable ardour of his hope droop for a moment. Rising aloft, even from the wild waste which men had made of their powers in all times past, he poured down the floods of his indignation upon those who are thus ready and willing to devote mankind to darkness and despair. Inspired by his philosophy, and pursuing his method, the more than immortal Newton did not fear, cautiously yet boldly, humbly yet hopefully, to pry into "the wonderful art" wherewith the Almighty has constructed the heavens; and the great problem which Socrates had so timidly, yet so rashly, pronounced to lie beyond the reach of man, did this humble student of nature most triumphantly solve; showing, to the admiration of the world and the glory of God, that that wonderful art is infinitely more wonderful than any thing which had ever been dreamed of in the philosophy of antiquity. How great soever, then, the failure of times past may have been, we should not despair. Nor should we listen, for a moment, to those who are ever ready to declare, that the great problem of the intellectual system of the universe is not within the reach of the human faculties.